ZOMBIE PUNKS FUCK OFF

Edited by

SAM RICHARDS

CONTENTS

Introduction by Sam Richard   v

While My Guitar Gently Eats   1

Hard-Wired Beat   11

Re-Made   19

The Ballad of Hank XXX   33

Eat the Rich   43

The Advent of Noise   53

The Good Samaritans   61

Earworm   73

Cyberpunk Zombie Jihad   87

I Am the Future   97

Rolled Up   107

Bass Sick   115

The Basement People   125

Nature Unveiled   137

About The Editor & Authors   149

Also by CLASH Books   153

INTRODUCTION BY SAM RICHARD

In the midst of working on Zombie Punks Fuck Off, my wife, Mo Richard, had an aortic aneurysm and died suddenly at 31. Obviously, my life came to a horrible, grinding stop, as did everything around me, including this book.

What strikes me most is how wrongly funny this book became following her death. It hurts more than words, but the irony is delicious. Mo loved horror and zombies; she loved punk and metal and gothy stuff. This was her shit. But to be working on a book about rising hordes of undead punks at the time of her death, when all I wanted was for her to come back to us, well, just know that she would approve of the absurdity.

Her support for me was ever-present, and this book was no exception; just like all the Weirdpunk Books - she illustrated the covers for the companion zines to both Blood for You and Hybrid Moments. She often pushed me to write more, to do more, and to fight against the depression. She was also the person I most wanted by my side in the event of a zombie apocalypse, or any variety of apocalypse, really. Another irony is that she can't fight off hordes of zombie with me in the future, like we often imagined; she'd be among their ranks.

This is a book filled with amazing stories by amazing authors conjuring worlds where punks and zombies collide; a pair that go together as perfectly as any over-used cliché can conjure. I couldn't let it sit unfinished. The stories were assembled; the authors had already done edits. Seriously, the contributors to this book are fucking incredible people and I wish to thank them for their understanding and compassion. This book needed to be completed. She would want the world to see it. And she would have loved it.

She and I always told each other that whoever died first was sworn to haunt the other, and yet I have seen no ghost. With the spirit of this book in mind, I'd like to imagine that she's gathering the ranks and forcing them to rise. Then, I could see her again, get to feel her touch once more, succumb to the oblivion that awaits us all, and her beautiful mouth could tear into my body; finally we could be together, forever - as we always dreamed.

For Maureen (Mo) Rose Richard (October 7, 1985 – August 13, 2017)

I await your return.

WHILE MY GUITAR GENTLY EATS

DANGER SLATER

Our guitarist is dead.

He killed himself 20 minutes ago. The rest of us only found out because his mom made this long-winded post about it on Facebook.

"Our little Chucky is at peace now," her post said, among other things. "Heaven just gained itself another angel."

It was real stupid shit, what she was writing. Chuck never believed in Heaven or Hell or God or Fate or any of that nonsense. None of us did. None of us believed in anything. We were nihilists. We did drugs and tried to get laid and played our music loud and fast because life was pointless and what the hell else were we supposed to do?

Pete left a comment on the Facebook post calling Chuck's mom a dumb cunt, and we all had a good laugh over that. She predictably freaked out and replied with this long chain of comments in which she basically blamed us for his death.

"Chucky was such a nice boy until he met all of you!" she said.

Yeah, lady, like we came over to your house and FORCED your son to drink a bottle of drain cleaner...

In the grand scheme of things, a dead guitarist wasn't really that big of a deal. It wasn't like having a broken amp, which could cost a lot of money to fix. Guitarists died all the time. That's why there was so damn many of them. When you're in a band and your guitarist dies, you just get someone else to take their place. There's no shortage of shitty musicians in the world.

Our band was called The Franz Liszts, named after a 19th century Hungarian composer who played the piano real good. Don't ask me to name a Franz Liszt song though, because I can't. All I know is that in his lifetime, Liszt was regarded as a musical genius. Our band name was meant to be ironic.

Am I worried about dying too, like Chuck?

Not really. I'm the singer for The Franz Liszts, but I'm also the bass player. Singers tend to die a lot, but bass players hardly ever die. I figured the two would even each other out, giving me a 50/50 chance of not making it through the rest of the day. Same odds as anyone else.

The guy replacing our dead guitarist for tonight's show was a real creep.

His name was Murr, which he claimed was short for Murder, even though I saw his driver's license once and it said his real name was Murray.

When Murr showed up at my house earlier, he was already drunk, smelling like vomit and unwashed armpits. Pete said something to him about it and he told us that he was so punk rock that he was going to kill all of us on stage and disembowel us and feed our flesh to his guitar. We weren't sure what he meant by that, until he took his guitar out of its case and held it up for Pete and me to see.

The body of the instrument was grey and soft, like flayed skin, stretched out to tan. There was a random eyeball, near the volume knob, rolling around in its bloodshot socket, watching this scene unfold, and a set of ears placed horizontally on the top part of the neck. And there was also a mouth, located right behind the bridge that looked like a human mouth, but a little bit bigger, and full of rotten yellow teeth. He strummed the strings and the mouth started salivating and moving up and down, like it was chewing, even though there was nothing for it to chew on.

"It's a zombie guitar," Murr said. "It eats meat. People meat. If I try to play it an' don't feed it proper, bad things happen."

"That's a load a' bullshit," said Pete. "Yer being a dumb cunt."

If Chuck's mom knew that Pete called everyone 'a dumb cunt' she probably wouldn't have gotten so upset before. Oh well.

"I'm not being dumb," he said. "That's just how it is. That's how it's always been."

I shook my head and scoffed, doubting very much that Murr was going to try to disembowel us, even if he wanted to. His name was Murray, for fuck's sake. That was such a nerdy name. I bet he couldn't even peel a juicy-looking grapefruit, let alone pull the guts out of the stomach of a human man.

We were in my garage, loading our equipment into the van.

We called our van the Vinny Van Go, after the famous painter Vincent van Gogh, who was apparently a genius like Franz Liszt, but who, unlike Liszt, was completely unappreciated in his time. The story goes that before he died he only sold one painting. For some reason people were supposed to find that inspiring.

Chuck once showed me a Vincent van Gogh painting on his computer. It was of a crooked black tower against the night sky, surrounded by all these swirling zephyrs and yellow stars. *The Starry Night* was what the painting was called.

He clicked the little box to maximize the picture, so that it took up the entire computer screen. He told me to sit in the chair and look at it for a few minutes.

"What th' fuck do I want to look at a dumb painting like this for?" I said to him.

"For the aesthetics," he quickly said back to me.

"Okay, but what th' fuck do I care about aesthetics?" I said.

"Because aesthetics are supposed to make you feel things," he replied. "Because you're an artist too, even if you don't want to admit it. We all are. And art begets art, like some kind of chronic disease passed down from generation to generation."

But what he was trying to say was totally lost on me because I knew Chuck was an idiot long before he drank all that drain cleaner and proved it. I once saw him smash a bottle against his head for two dollars. Shards of glass were sticking out of his skull, and blood ran down his face and in between the cracks in his blissfully stupid grin. It was fucking disgusting. He was dead now and his opinion was moot. Still, from that day on, I always wondered what he was talking about, why he made me sit there, and why he called me an artist. Nobody ever called me an artist. I couldn't sing. Hell, I didn't even try to sing. Normally, I'd just scream into the microphone, as loud and obnoxious as I could. One show I was so fucked up I forgot every word to every song and instead I just yelled a bunch of racial slurs at people in the audience. I didn't know if my bass was in tune most of the time, and truth was, I really didn't care. The thing about The Franz Liszts was we weren't concerned with boring shit like tempo. Or rhythm. If you want to dance, you could go put on a fucking Bee Gees record. If you came to one of our shows it was probably because you hated yourself as much as I did.

I asked Murr how his guitar become a zombie.

"That's not a normal thing to happen to guitars," I said. "Most of them are jus' made of wood."

"Yeah, they all start out as wood." Murr scoffed. "Some people wanna act like its black magic, like I sold my soul to the devil or something like that, but both you and I know there ain't no devils at work here, and there's no such things as souls."

"So what's the deal then?" I said. "How could this'a happened?"

"I used to play with these dudes a couple a' months ago," he said. "Real good musicians, these guys were. Best I've ever seen, at least. The one dude, he'd play his guitar like he was possessed. He'd close his eyes, move his fingers, and he'd just disappear. It was like tuning a radio, and the music was just comin' outta him.

"They had zombie instruments too, these guys. A zombie bass and zombie drums and a zombie microphone for the singer to sing in. That's parta the reason they played so good. Zombie instruments always sound the best. Problem was, they didn't feed 'em proper. Didn't give them the sacrifice they demanded. Maybe they didn't know that that's what you were supposed to do, if you wanted to keep on playing. That their instruments demanded new flesh to sustain them.

"Anyway, I go over there for rehearsals one day, and the garage is empty. Lights were on and everything was still plugged in. There was feedback coming through one of the amps, a high-pitched electric buzz that felt like a wasp inside of my ears. I figured they were on a beer run or out scorin' some dope or whatever. They'd be back any minute.

"Their zombie instruments were still there, of course. Mouths moving up and down. The drum set had a few chunks of wobbly fat between its teeth and clumps of blood-soaked hair running down its cheeks. The bass snarled and snapped at me when I got too close. That's when it dawned to me. They weren't running no errands; they had all been eaten. I probably shoulda been more worried, 'bout getting eaten myself, but I was suddenly struck with this…impulse. There was this song, waiting to be written, and it just popped into my head like it had been hiding there all along, an' I just happened to find it. So I sat down and started playing around, strumming a few chords, and goddamn if it didn't sound halfway decent for once. I certainly didn't know it at the time, but it was right then that the infection had spread to my guitar."

Even though I still thought his stupid story was bullshit, I found myself saying:

"Dude, fuck that noise! This shit is dangerous. We need to kill it. We need to kill your guitar. We need to stab it right through the heart before it comes for us like it did for them. Does your guitar even have a heart? How would we stop it?"

Murr sighed. "Listen, everyone wants to act like there ain't no new ideas left in the world. That all the thoughts have already been thunk and every note I could possibly play on this thing has already been plucked. Well, maybe I don't like that. Maybe I'm the only motherfucker left out here trying to create something new. You want to kill it? I don't think you can. It's a lot bigger than us. This ain't a hobby, dude. It's a fucking curse."

The gig that night was in an old bomb shelter, right off the main strip in town. People called it The Meatlocker even though it technically didn't have a name. It was located underneath the fancy French restaurant that the rich people in town liked to eat at on special occasions. To get into The Meatlocker you had to go through an unmarked doorway in the rear of the building. This door was the only way in or out of the venue. If there was ever a fire down there everyone would burn up and die.

The walls of The Meatlocker were made of concrete, thick and cold, covered in stickers and graffiti; EAT COCK in thick, black Sharpie, scribbled on top of a Bad Religion sticker that had probably been slapped there back in 1992. The people dining in the restaurant above couldn't hear what we were doing down there, no matter how loud the music was. They'd only see all the punks hanging out in the alley, smoking cigarettes and smashing empty beer bottles and fucking behind the dumpster.

There was no stage in The Meatlocker. Bands just played in the far corner of the room.

"Is there a bathroom in here?" I heard some kid ask the girl who collected the money at the bottom of the stairs. She handed him a bucket and told him to dump it outside when he was done.

I drank half a fifth of vodka and split a blunt with Pete and Murr.

We were ready to play.

"Hey, we're The Franz Liszts and here's a song that you're probably gonna hate," I slurred into the microphone.

Pete clicked his drumsticks four times, faster than machine gun fire, 1-2-3-4, and then it was pretty much just a wall of noise after that – angry and loud and out-of-tune and violent – and all the kids in The Meatlocker danced around and bobbed their heads and beat the shit out of each other like it was the only thing they were born to do. And, in that moment, it was.

I couldn't stop looking at Murr's guitar, though. The lips on the mouth on it kept flopping up and down, almost like it was trying to sing along with me. I got so hypnotized by it that I forgot the words to the song I was singing.

"*Gnnah fffattth bbabbmeb smathh, rrefth aaf oopfthah haatt.*"

I screamed that and a bunch of other garbled nonsense and nobody seemed to notice or care.

Murr looked like a crazy person, but not like a wear-your-underwear-on-the-outside-of-your-pants kind of crazy person. His craziness was much more subtle.

He was making this serious-looking face, like he was trying to remember something, like he was doing math in his head and concentrating really hard on it. He stood with his legs spread apart and his back hunched over, his zombie guitar slung low between his knees. Greasy sweat ran down his acne scarred forehead, slithering around pockmarks like rainwater down a muddy windshield. When he looked back at me, there was fire in his eyes. His pupils seemed to be swirling like those stupid stars in that van Gogh painting.

He hit a power C and let it ring out, but only for a moment, because his fingers began pirouetting their way up and down the neck. Note after note, he played, in perfect harmony, as clear and crisp as a remastered CD. He was playing a solo. A fucking guitar solo.

I looked at Pete. His nostrils were flared and his eyebrows were scrunched up into a W, as if to say "what the fuck?" to me, because what the fuck, indeed. The Franz Listzs didn't have guitar solos. We didn't even have a guitarist. He died that morning.

Pete, not knowing what else to do at this point, just shrugged, put his head down, and attempted to match his drumming to Murr's manic finger-plucking. It took a few seconds, but eventually their tempos lined up. They fell into sync. They were jamming. And it sounded surprisingly good.

Well, shit, I thought. *I'll be damned if I'mma let these two assholes show me up an' make me look like some sorta fuckin' noob. Now how's this thing work…*

And so I did something I never did before either. I played my bass, like, *actually* played it. To the best of my ability, at least. And I sung my lyrics too. I sung the words loud and clear, so that everyone could make out what I was saying.

And, just like that, we were making music together. I couldn't believe how easy it had come.

That's when I looked down and saw that my bass had transformed into a zombie too.

The paint had gone sallow and the body had gone from cedar wood to rotten flesh. A mouth had appeared beneath strings, its sticky black tongue licking against my knuckles as I played.

But not just that: the neck itself became an arm – a bicep, elbow, and forearm – with a hand at the far end of it, an open palm with long yellow nails on the tip of each finger. The hand wiggled, perhaps as confused by its sudden appearance as I was. But it didn't remain confused for long, because the arm swung back around and grabbed me by the hair. The strings on the bass all strained, then snapped in half, whipping around like jellyfish tentacles.

Before I could react, the mouth bit into my fingers. I screamed into the microphone, but the tip of that had turned into a mouth too and it screamed back at me and clamped down, tearing my lips off my head. My exposed teeth were forced into a permanent clown grin as skin hung limp from my hemorrhaging jaw. The mic then ate that too, like my old man used to eat the skin off a chicken at KFC. The microphone ate my entire face off of my skull. I couldn't even close my eyes to shield myself from the horror, as I had no eyelids anymore.

I turned my head to see Pete's legs straight up in the air, perpendicular to the floor, his arms flailing around helplessly as he was sucked down into the maw of his own ravenous zombie drum kit. Blood poured out from the hole in the kick, a syrupy puddle of red washing its way out into the sea of Converse sneakers and Doc Martin boots. There was no drain on the floor of The Meatlocker. The crowd stood ankle deep in blood.

Murr kept playing the longest out of the three of us. Maybe because he knew it would end like this. Every time he strummed his strings the mouth on his bridge took another chunk out of his hand. After a while, his entire right arm was stripped down to just bone, a creepy flesh-stippled skeleton appendage playing a punk rock funeral dirge to the handful of horrified kids still left in the room.

I was losing consciousness now. I had fallen over and my bass was eating me from the ankles up. It was consuming me, wholly.

The pain wasn't really registering, probably from shock, so I didn't really mind as it chewed its way past my waist, my guts spilling out of my stomach all around me.

I guess I did get disemboweled, after all.

Murr's guitar took a large bite out of his side and his chest cavity opened up, his heart rolling out from under his ribs and onto the floor. Pete had already been eaten, the drums swallowing him almost in one gulp. Still, I clawed at my bass's broken strings and attempted to gurgle out the last of the lyrics, mostly to no avail. I couldn't tell you why I was trying to finish the song instead of just dying like I was about to anyway. It was almost like I didn't have a choice. It was almost like it wasn't me who was playing the music, but the music that was playing through me.

I looked out at what was left of the audience. Most of them had left, ran away, screaming, puking, crying for help. Others just looked on in abject terror, frozen like statues. My brain wasn't working right anymore. My thoughts were sinking away like pirate ships that had been struck by cannonballs and all the notions by which I referred to *me* as *myself* were fading into permanent black oblivion. It was not unlike being drunk, truth be told.

Anyway, before I bade farewell to the pointless parade of days I called my life, I started to laugh. Riotously laugh, actually, like I just heard the funniest joke ever told. It was a dead man's laugh, of course, full of phlegm and sadness, but it echoed throughout my chest nonetheless, loud and long and free. And as the world disappeared around me, I could only think that in a lot of ways, I was kind of like Franz Liszt. Or, perhaps I was more like Vincent van Gogh. Either way, you were a part of my captive audience, weren'tcha? You saw everything. You were my witness. And what I just created...well, I guess you'd have no choice but to call it art.

HARD-WIRED BEAT

BY AXEL KOHAGEN

The dead air felt like heat lighting and old secrets. Dwayne wondered if either of them would touch down in his bar.

Iowa's most famous musician walked into the bar after the young, talented band already packed up and left after their set. The band called itself 112(Lonely). It used to be their t-shirts were more artistic than their songs, but the band's keyboardist recently turned a corner and wrote songs that stood out from the mediocre college bands they shared stages with. And maybe it wasn't such bad luck she missed the state's most famous musician. She'd see him again; he was, after all, her father.

"You just missed her," Dwayne said. "The band's down to a duo now, but they sound great. She might be as good as her dad."

Peter Balance stomped about the bar like he didn't hear Dwayne. He looked over the stage like his daughter Jaye might be hiding in the cracks. Dwayne didn't worry about him scaring away his customers. Three of them were pounding pitchers and celebrating their friend's purchase of a boat. The other two were committed alcoholics who would man their benches until the trumpet of judgment day sounded.

"Her car's out front," Peter said.

"She rode with her bandmate?" Dwayne asked.

"I'm going to need to go down to your basement," Peter said.

"Don't think you 'need' to do that," Dwayne said. His drunks pricked up their ears.

"They're out, Dwayne," he said. "If they're still down there, they might accept me instead of her. But if they're out and got her already . . ."

"Who did what?" Dwayne asked.

"Boat! Boat! Boat! Boat!" the table of men cheered.

"I'm going down there," Peter said. However, despite the creepy tattoos peeking out from his sleeves and collar, he was a small man in comparison to Dwayne and the drunks looked like they might throw in a beating just for good measure.

"Quickly," Peter said. "Listen carefully. Do you remember when I wasn't a solo act?"

Initially, Peter barely made an impact on his own band. They started out as C&M, because they thought they'd get sued if they went by the proper name of the popular snack food. Any time he tried to change the mood of a song with a unique keyboard line, lead guitarist Mike Parsons stopped him quickly. Rozz Venable, the drummer, seemed interested in taking the band in a new direction, and bassist Ward Jefferson didn't seem to care about music composition or anything else.

Both members of his rhythm section were often distracted by other life issues. Rozz gave birth to a little girl two months before Halloween. She never said whose child it was, but Ward spent a lot of time in her house helping her out. Ward and his friend Jim Shepherd, whom he brought everywhere. If Rozz weren't so focused on the kid, she'd side with Peter and C&M could go from being a nondescript grunge band into something with teeth.

They were seniors in their various high schools, and they wouldn't be attending the same college. Peter had half a school year to put together at least a decent single so he could round up his real band in college. He had half a mind to kick Mike out and sequence the guitars on his synthesizer, but Ward was such a pacifist wuss he'd stop coming to practice if Peter ever raised the drama level.

"Tomorrow?" Peter asked as his band fled the basement of a local bar. He still hadn't seen a dime from any of them for the studio rental, but they had the nerve to roll their eyes like he was the asshole.

"Yeah," Ward said. "Tomorrow."

"Say hi to the kid," Peter said, and Rozz shot him a look he felt the whole drive home.

"You're saying you left some practice stuff in there about twenty years ago and you have to have it right now? This second?" Dwayne said. He positioned himself between the basement door and the frazzled musician. His right hand dropped to gently touch the rounded end of a baseball bat.

"It has value," Peter said.

"Titties!" yelled one of the people at the boat table.

"You had one good song, 'Cask,'" Dwayne said. "That was fifteen years ago. How valuable can any of your old shit be?"

"'Cask' sells enough every year that I don't have to work ever again," Peter said. "Even after file sharing. Julliard has taught it in grad courses for over decade."

"What a fucking asshole!" said one of the guys at the bar.

"Anyway, what reason do you have to keep me from going down there?" Peter said.

"I know you kicked your daughter out when she started playing better than you," Dwayne said. "I know she stole your old synthesizer for tonight's show because she still loves you for some ridiculous reason. And I have a hunch that's what you want to get back."

"Oh shit," Peter said. "She played my synthesizer?"

Behind Dwayne, the door to the basement blew open.

They never found the rest of C&M after their final practice. They found Ward's car at the airport's long-term parking, and that was it. Their families held vigils every year for three years, and then they moved the mourning inside and kept living life.

It took Peter longer than he expected to compare his DNA to Jaye, Rozz's daughter. The results were exactly as he expected, and he took her from Rozz's parents and raised her like a fragile but poisonous princess. Years later, he found out Ward's friend Jim had been Ward's boyfriend for all of high school.

In those early days, after he finally got Jaye to sleep, he went to his synthesizer for hours on end. He pulled up files and loops and samples from his own special stash. He mixed the track over and over again, until he found himself with a nine minutes and thirty-two second industrial symphony of metal corroding and conquering flesh. When he finished and listened to it, he shivered so mightily he covered up in two blankets on a summer's night.

The first thing through the door was big and hollow, like a wasp's nest of decaying flesh. Rats and mice took to these holes and, as the big thing moved, they scampered from hole to hole nervously, unused to being disrupted. The human head atop this shambling creature flopped forward and back, as if only secured by a string.

"What the fuck is that?" Dwayne asked. He grabbed his baseball bat and stepped away from the approaching monster. The monster, in turn, held the door open for friends.

A small corpse gently made its way up the stairs. This zombie had to walk carefully, because all it had for feet were bony nubs. Its hands were worn to nubs as well, and it walked with them at its side like a penguin waddles. Her dead face was all sag and empty eyes.

The boat table turned to see these things step into the bar. None of them had anything to cheer now. The two drunks at the bar ran out the back door.

Behind her came the noisiest beast of all, its steps forming a subtle, stable pattern that kept a beat. It walked with one foot hammering into the floor, and then an elongated left arm taking the next step instead of a foot. It had to move this way; its remaining arm and leg were no longer there. Its head lay against its chest. When it got all the way up the stairs, the smallest zombie began tapping its arm bones together, creating a beat to match the loud footsteps of its friend. Then, the biggest of them screamed.

The boat table walked toward these things like it was any old bar fight. The biggest zombie held the first two heroes to the holes in its chest. They screamed and the rats inside the dead body squeaked as they tore into the eyes, noses, and ears of men who soon wouldn't care who owned a boat. When the behemoth dropped them, one had a rat wiggling down his throat.

The tiny zombie leaped on the next drunk boater. She knocked him down and sat on him, and then her bony forearms did their work. They stabbed into the man's chest and throat with quick, precise motions. He filled the floor with blood quickly, but he took much longer to die.

The last one died quickest. The big, gawky thing sat down and used its giant arm like a whip. Dwayne could hear the customer's neck snap and then watched it bobble around like a carnival game as the man fell to the floor.

"Peter," the smallest one said. Her voice sounded full of mud, pain, and sorrow.

It turned out he could convince Mike of anything if he told him he'd get laid because of it, and after that Rozz and Ward joined right in. The question was – how far would they go?

"I'm not wearing this," Ward said.

"Trust me," Peter said. "This is how we get the right sound. Bands do this stuff all the time. They play in a different environment to bring out different sounds from the instruments."

"This isn't a different environment," Ward said. He held up two heavy canvas packs with weights sowed in to them.

"It's a different mindset," Peter explained. Your put one on your right arm and one on your left leg to throw your balance off. The harder you work will make your playing sounded strained, difficult. Like living in a world of machines and no humanity."

"We all liked those first bands you liked, "Mike said. "But the weird stuff you got into is where you lost us. Like that Eeny-Meeny Mo-baton. Nobody really likes that."

"I know," Peter said. His smile was so forced his cheeks

throbbed. "That's why you guys agreed to try this just the once, as a favor to me"

Rozz got behind her kit and Peter strapped her in. He told her he wanted a giant sound from her, and she'd have to fight for it as the chains and bungee cords held her in place.

"Mine is just too dangerous," Mike said. He poked at the circular saw hanging in the air in front of him with a pointer finger. "You really think you're going to turn this thing on and let it hang in front of me while I'm playing."

"You always want to sound edgier," Peter said.

"I'll be right outside the room," Peter said when everything was just so. "I need it quiet so I can get the levels right. I want you to improvise with each other. Just let the mood hit you and go with it. Remember, you only have to do this once. I mean, unless it really works for you."

Peter stepped outside and locked the door. He set up his equipment to record everything, and then he knocked three times on the door so they would start playing. They improvised while he made sure their practice area was sealed watertight. After they played for five minutes, he turned on the water and filled up the practice space until all three of them drowned.

"Okay, fuck it," Dwayne said. He staggered backward on shaking knees.

"They've been down there the whole time," Peter said. He laughed at the oncoming, undead members of his former band. He reached into his front pocket.

His old bassist stopped and began stomping in place. His foot and long, distorted arm alternated their assaults on the floor, forming a bouncy but serious bass line. Rozz tapped her bone-arms atop each other in a heated, high-hat rhythm. Mike howled like a dying dog, but his mournful melody was not lost amidst the terror.

"You take three mediocre musicians and record their slow, complicated deaths and you get yourself a hit song you can live off of," Peter said. "Even if you find out that's the only good idea you're ever going to have. And now look at them! They're much more interesting musicians swollen and dead!"

"Are you coming or what?" Dwayne asked. He held the back door open, but Peter finally found the cellphone he was looking for in his pocket. He fumbled with the unlock screen. Dwayne screamed from deep in his chest, and Peter winced because the sound ruined the music he was hearing.

"You kidding me?" Peter said. "I need to record this. I might have a second song in me after all."

Rozz took a few steps forward. Peter finally unlocked his phone, amidst Rozz tapping out a furious solo of sorts. Peter grimaced and flipped through screens. Rozz stopped her tapping and drove one of her bone-arms straight through his eye and into his brain.

Dwayne ran screaming into the night.

—————

Jaye sat smoking a joint at her bandmate's house to celebrate their successful first gig.

"How pissed is your dad going to be when he finds out you stole his old synth?" Brock Davis said.

"Less pissed than when he finds out I have more talent than him," Jaye said. "When I re-used his old stuff I could feel it change. Like something in the building woke up, you know."

"Phone's ringing," Brock said.

"Speak of the devil," Jaye said. "Dad."

Jaye answered her phone. Her brow furrowed. She pointed to Brock's phone and gestured frantically until he tossed it to her.

"What is it?" Brock asked.

"It's a song," Jaye said. "It sounds like Dad screaming, but there's a song underneath it. Maybe he isn't so mad at me after all."

"Is the song any good?" Brock asked.

"I think so," Jaye said. She turned on the speaker so Brock could hear the screaming. Jaye found the recording app on the phone and preserved the song for later. "Listen to him scream! He's really getting into it!"

RE-MADE

BY MADISON MCSWEENEY

For my current circumstances, I can only thank the Decency in Commerce Commission of America.

Had it not been for their glorious crusade to stop rock and roll from poisoning the young minds of America, I would never have been arrested outside a record store in Scranton, Pennsylvania, I would never have ended up at the Parrish Center for Sub-Cultural Youth, and I certainly would not be writing this with my left arm.

But whatever.

At the Center, one of the first things they taught us was to let go of the past. Don't look back at who you were, at what you *might* have been had you been permitted to live unimpeded; don't even look at what you are *now*. The best course of action is to look towards the future.

At my current rate of composition, I have about six months of future to look forward to, before my body has completely rotted away and I'm left a gibbering mass of flesh and bone for my fellow upstanding citizens to consume.

I don't know who, if anyone, will ever read this. I imagine after the outbreak is dealt with, one way or another, there will be an investigation, and that investigation will lead them back to the Center and to this document.

Unless, of course, the plague *doesn't* get dealt with.

———

The year was 1992 (I guess it still is, but I digress). The Ramones album *Brain Drain* had just come out - three years behind schedule, due to bureaucratic dickering by the DICCs of America over what age-restriction to put on it (I imagine Johnny must have been driven up the wall).

The day in question was a Saturday in early October. The air was still unseasonably warm, but occasionally an icy gust of wind would wrap itself around you and worm its way underneath your clothes, making you think you'd been groped by a ghost. The trees – the few that were left in the inner suburbs – bled red and orange.

I'd just finished a shift at the local Burger King, and was loitering around Deadman Records before heading home. Half the shelves were empty; as per local obscenity bylaws, anything with potentially offensive cover art was stored out-of-sight. If you wanted to buy one of those albums, you had to locate it in the store catalogue and ask at the counter.

I don't know what possessed me to ask if they had *Brain Drain* in stock, but the beleaguered hippie who ran the place made such a production of digging the album out of storage that I felt compelled to shell out and buy it.

The DICCs had given the record a 16+ rating (the standard restriction slapped on any punk or metal album, in order to keep such materials out of the hands of the vulnerable). I was only fifteen, but had a fake ID for those purposes. The forged driver's license, which identified me as nineteen-year-old Brad Constantinatikos from California instead of fifteen-year-old Brett Campbell from Pennsylvania, was of admittedly substandard quality. However, the old stoner at the counter was nearly blind and didn't really care; I would have purchased the album and brought it home without incident had a DICC Compliance Inspector not shown up just as I was walking out of the store.

The DICC inspector was a middle-aged bureaucrat-type with a patchy comb over and a suspicious moustache that was thicker than his head hair. He looked so utterly disinterested that, at first, I thought he was just going to let me keep walking. However, right before I was about to pass him by, he raised his hand and motioned for me to hand over my bag.

In addition to the 16+ label stamped onto the album cover itself, the record included a black-and-white sticker with the word DOGS, an acronym indicating the adult content contained within. D was for Drugs, O for Occult, G was for Anti-Government Sentiment and S was Sex. The joke among my circles was that no album was worth buying if it didn't have at least one DOG on the cover

He looked at me again. "May I see your identification?"

I tried to smile in a casual manner, but I don't think it worked. "Of course, sir," I said, handing over my Constantinatikos ID.

The Inspector looked at the ID, glanced back at me, eyed my dyed green hair and the line of rings snaking up the cartilage of my left ear, and then looked back down at the ID card. He studied it for a long while before raising his head again. He met my eyes for a good five seconds before blurting out, "You don't look Greek."

When my deeply respectable parents arrived at the police station, I was sitting in a holding cell with my hands cuffed behind my back.

"Acquiring fraudulent government ID for the purposes of contravening Decency in Commerce legislation is a very serious charge," the first cop told my mother, who was struggling to restrain tears.

The second cop shook his head. "Of course, this sort of disregard for public institutions is typical among youths like your son."

"And what is that supposed to mean?" replied my father, who had been taking a nap when the police called and still didn't quite have his wits about him.

The cop made a show of hesitating and groping for the most tactful word and coming out with a word salad. "Practitioners of the... 'punk' movement."

At this epithet, my parents looked at me in unison. They

noted my dyed green hair, the line of holes snaking up the cartilage of my left ear (the police had taken the liberty of removing
my piercings during booking), and my general disregard for
public institutions, and finally put two-and-two together.

The police were very civil to my despondent parents and, in a
display of the benevolent mercy of the justice system, agreed to
let me off with a warning.

"That said," said the first officer as he removed my cuffs, "we
have some materials here that you may want to take a look at."
His partner handed my father a glossy brochure with blue text on
a grey background. From my place in the holding cell, I couldn't
make out the title, but noticed that the front cover featured a
smiling young man with a crew cut and khaki pants.

I waited anxiously while my parents studied the document
with a grim sincerity. After several minutes, the first cop piped
up again: "We have an informational video for you, if this
program intrigues you." Without waiting for confirmation, he
nodded to his partner, who disappeared into a back room and
returned wheeling out a television monitor hooked up to a VCR.
He popped in a tape, and after a moment of whiteness and fuzz,
Jerry Parrish appeared on the screen.

I suddenly felt deeply unsafe.

So here's the deal.

Jerry Parrish used to be one of us – the worst of us, some
would say. Slightly before my time, he'd been the face of a band
called The Pigs, known as much for obscene stunts involving effi-
gies of sitting politicians as their distinctive brand of left-leaning
lyrics.

Parrish was equal parts artist and activist, an anti-authori-
tarian anarchist who would aim his ire at any element of society
that displeased him. For a while, he was the conscience of the
punk movement – one of the sole defenses we had against self-
indulgence, stagnation and commercial co-optation. One day,
Parrish went too far. In the middle of a show in some side-road

strip mall bar in Slaterville, New Jersey, the Secret Service burst in and arrested him for obscenity and sedition.

The moron insisted on making a mockery of the judicial process. He acted as his own lawyer, even though everyone knew he had the money to hire a proper one; he showed up to the first day of the trial with duct tape over his mouth; he repeatedly referred to the (male) judge as "Her Majesty."

Of course, he was convicted. The judge could have sent him to the electric chair, but, in a display of the benevolent mercy of the justice system, decided that Parrish should be given a second chance. He could be re-made as an upright, contributing member of society, if he could only be made to understand the error of his ways.

Jerry went away for a while. He emerged several years later, a different person.

Memories of his trial still fresh in their minds, the media came out in droves to his press conference. Parrish came onstage wearing a beige suit, his prematurely graying hair neatly parted at the side. He explained that he'd spent the past three years at a government rehabilitation centre in Nevada, and that, with the help of the best specialists the government had to offer, he had come to realize that the punk movement had brainwashed him. Its anti-government, anti-institutional sentiment, and the anti-social actions it inspired, was deeply unhealthy. He regretted his actions and wanted to make amends.

"From this moment on, I have a new purpose," he said gravely. "I want to help others who have been deceived like I was." Borrowing therapeutic techniques he had learned from the U.S. government, he explained, he would open a center dedicated to turning troubled youths into upright, contributing members of society.

"I'm a new man," he concluded. "I've been re-made, and now I want to help others remake themselves."

My parents watched raptly as a videotape version of Jerry Parrish took them on a tour of the sprawling facilities of the Parrish Center for Sub-Cultural Youth.

The bunker-like buildings were made of grey concrete; the

few aerial shots of the compound showed nothing but trees for miles around. Inside, the facilities were austere but modern. In addition to what Parrish called a "state-of-the-art vocational curriculum," students were assigned work details to help with the upkeep of the facility.

In one particularly painful scene, Parrish exchanged canned dialogue with a young woman spooning what looked like dog food into white plastic bowls.

"What's on the menu today, Michelle?"

The girl smiled at the camera. "Beef stroganoff – my secret recipe!"

Parrish laughed as the girl continued to smile. It was a dancer's smile – plastered on like paint, not quite reaching the eyes. "Three months ago, you would never have seen this young lady in a kitchen," Parrish explained. "Michelle was hanging around with bad people, associating with radical political movements, and had convinced herself that domestic duties were somehow demeaning."

"I certainly was silly back then, Jerry," Michelle replied. "Now I can't wait to go home and cook for my family every day."

"I'm sure they can't wait, either," Parrish concluded, resting a hand on her shoulder before turning to face the camera again.

"This is the kind of change that you can expect in your child after a short time at the Parrish Center." He pursed his lips into a kind of sympathetic grimace. "I won't lie to you – it's tough raising kids these days, with so many anti-social social movements trying to suck them in." He smiled winsomely. His teeth were very straight and very white.

"I was on the inside of the punk rock movement, and I know how to get kids out of it. Utilizing government approved rehabilitation techniques, I can soften the hardcore, quell the riot grrls, and put a dent in the straight-edgers."

It struck me that those puns would go over the head of parents; I wondered if that last line wasn't designed to send a chill through future students.

There was another dramatic aerial shot of the facility, before the camera returned to the ground and zoomed in on Parrish's taut face.

"Send your troubled child to the Parrish Centre for Sub-Culture Youths," he concluded. "They'll come out new."

"I beg of you," I said, for the fifth time the morning of my departure, "Please reconsider."

I got down on my knees as my dad reluctantly looked up from his paper. "I'll change on my own. I'll be the best-behaved kid you could ever dream of."

My father shook his head. "I don't like this any more than you do, Brett. But we're out of options. You've fallen in with bad influences."

"I have not!" I cried. "I'm my own person."

"That's exactly the problem. Every man has to conform to some extent, if he wants to make anything of his life. You haven't learned that yet."

I was incredulous. "I'm fifteen!"

"And going nowhere!"

I flinched back, startled.

"Look at you!" he continued. "Your brother has an A-minus average and spent the summer interning at Lydon, Biafra and Associates. You're a C student at best, you're working part-time at Burger King, and you're spending all your spare time blasting that vulgar music. You're only fifteen and you're already falling behind."

My mother chimed in. "This Mr. Parrish was like you once – and now look at him."

Dad nodded. "I think this place will really straighten you out. You'll be a new man."

The Parrish Center bus came to pick me up at five o'clock that day. I'd packed a small bag, but the driver told me to leave it, as I wouldn't be needing anything at the Center.

I was the final addition to a small class of four unfortunate punks, three guys and a girl. The girl I recognized as the bassist in a local band – Beth something. Beth was seventeen-years-old and a staple at political demonstrations for whatever cause happened to roll into town. She'd gotten arrested for throwing a rock through a window during a demonstration protesting the unlawful arrest of another protester; like me, she'd been let off with a warning and had been shipped out by her parents.

The younger of the guys, Matt Sellers, had briefly gone to summer school with me before dropping out to join a commune upstate. Commune life, evidently, had not worked out – as he explained it, the leadership was insufficiently committed to the cause of societal liberation – so Matt decided to return home to his parents, who had other ideas on the matter. Matt had never been heavily involved in the punk scene, at least to my knowledge, but I suppose he was deviant enough for the new-and-improved Parrish to take on.

The last guy looked to be about twenty-eight years old; I assumed he was there on a court order rather than by parental coercion. He introduced himself as Mark Lobotomy (as we later found out, his real name was Marcus Lobomowitz, and we were not allowed to call him anything else). Marcus was also in a band (hence the stage name), but not one that got a lot of gigs. His facial features were almost completely obscured by piercings and his arms were covered in tattoos, including a grapefruit-sized portrait of Ronald Reagan on his right bicep. He ended up seated next to Beth on the bus, and they spent the duration of the trip in a heated argument.

The driver never told us exactly where the Center was located, but the bus ride took about four hours. When we arrived, we were greeted by a non-descript man in a grey suit who introduced himself as "Barlow," as well as a blonde woman in a pantsuit who didn't say anything at all.

The first thing Barlow did was pass around a square wooden box, into which he told us to deposit any piercings or jewelry. By the time the box reached me, it was heavy and rattling. I removed my nine cartilage piercings and handed the box back to him.

"Alright," he said. "Now all of you strip."

"What?" shouted Beth.

"You heard me."

Matt stammered. "Right here?"

"You got a problem with that, kid?" sneered Marcus, who was already undoing his belt.

"Well I certainly do," said Beth. "I'm not taking my clothes off out in the open like this."

Barlow nodded. "Of course. For the young lady, we have a room set aside. My associate will escort you." The female staffer nodded and gestured at Beth to follow her. It would be the last time any of us would see Beth for several days.

Barlow turned to us again and repeated his command. We stripped without protest. Once we were all down to our socks and underwear, he led us inside the main building, which opened into a large, open room with floor-to-ceiling mirrors and blinding white tiles.

The processing procedure was quick and dehumanizing. After changing into our grey uniforms, we were lined up behind a desk chair in the middle of the room and each given a haircut and an injection of a suspicious-looking purple fluid.

"Yo, what is this shit?" Marcus demanded as he was pricked.

"It's called Newfutrisol," Barlow replied, not averting his eyes from Ronald Reagan. "It will make you more amenable to our curriculum."

"Screw that," Marcus replied. "I won't be amenable to shit."

"We'll see about that." He looked away from Reagan. "Also, your tattoos are greatly inappropriate. We'll have them removed prior to graduation." He shoved Mark off the chair and motioned for me to take his place. I watched in horrified fascination as chunks of green hair dropped to the floor, but flinched away from the needle.

"I don't do drugs," I said.

Barlow grabbed my arm and jabbed it with the syringe. "You do now."

Over the next few days, we were treated to daily injections of Newfutrisol, in addition to what the staff called "individualized instruction."

The curriculum was different for each of us - Beth was taught the basics of home economics, including cooking, sewing, and dishwashing; Matt reported being forced to watch videos of business seminars and presidential speeches; Marcus, ironically, was subjected to what he called "Communist propaganda." The Center didn't teach me much of anything – instead, I got a daily dose of enough dope to leave me in a stupor for the rest of the day.

Occasionally, Parrish himself would stop by one of our sessions, and tell us how pleased he was with our progress.

"I don't understand the end game," I remarked one day over lunch. The meal was a meat loaf prepared by Beth, who was not yet the best cook, and I struggled to chew in between sentences. "What are they trying to do here?"

"It's right-wing indoctrination," Matt declared. "They're trying to re-make us into good little conservative capitalists so we can settle in nicely into their patriarchal hegemonic society."

Marcus, not looking up from the mess on his plate, shook his head. "Moron."

"Excuse me?"

"You're excused." He returned to picking at his meat loaf, but soon became agitated again and looked up at Matt. "Two reasons you're a moron. Firstly, capitalism is the greatest force for good ever to descend upon modern society."

This wasn't the brainwashing talking – Mark had been a right-winger long before his arrival at the Center, as he had told us repeatedly.

"I won't debate you on that because it would require a basic understanding of economics on your part," Marcus continued. "But if you think this is a right-wing project, you're an even bigger fool than I thought."

"What are you talking about?" Beth snapped.

Marcus paused to collect his thoughts, running a hand over what was left of his hair. "Don't you get it?" he finally said. "This isn't about left or right – it's about making you *not-you*. Beth's a feminist, so they're turning her into a homemaker. They're exposing Matt to Milton Friedman and me to Karl Marx."

He pointed at me. "They know you're straight-edge, so they're doping you up. If you were a user they'd detox you. It's all about making you what you aren't – taking every shred of individuality and stripping it away. Once you're not you any more, its easy to make you conform."

"Conform to what, though?" I asked.

"Who knows?" He pointed at Matt. "He's the big government fan – why don't you ask him what Big Brother's up to?"

The instant Matt lashed out, I was busy trying to saw the

rock-hard loaf with a butter knife, so I missed the punch. I looked up just in time to see Marcus falling backwards, his nose spewing blood like geyser. He wasn't on the ground for long though, and I think he would have beaten Matt into a pulp had Barlow and the other staffer not intervened.

Barlow took the liberty of restraining Matt, who was hysterical and close to tears, leaving his female associate the unenviable task of wrestling Marcus to the ground. Beth hopped up from her seat, and I thought a full-on brawl was about to break out, before the chaos was cut short by the subtle scent of smoke wafting in.

In unison, we all turned towards the source. Standing in the doorframe was Parrish, smoking a cigarette and watching the scene with a look of contempt.

Barlow was the first to break the silence. "Apologies, sir. We have the situation under control."

"You clearly don't," Parrish replied, his voice implacable. "Up his dosage of Newfutrisol."

Matt joined us again for lunch the next day, but he wasn't himself. At first, I thought he was just pissed off at Marcus, but eventually we realized that he was a vegetable. Parrish and his goons had loaded Matt with so much Newfutrisol that he could barely think, let alone talk.

His condition deteriorated every day. He was incoherent, and he stunk so badly that no one would have wanted to sit next to him even if he could converse. By the fifth day, his skin had taken on a greenish hue. I think Marcus felt partially responsible, because that day, he left our table to sit next to Matt.

Matt ignored him initially, so Marcus tried to goad him into conversation, insulting the Communist Manifesto and extolling the virtues of Reaganomics. After several minutes of this, Matt turned around and studied Marcus for well over thirty seconds, before leaning over and sinking his teeth into Marcus's shoulder.

Barlow and his partner had been increasingly vigilant since the first incident; the two staffers were able to subdue Matt easily, and within two minutes of the bite were dragging him off to solitary confinement. Marcus was left on the ground, howling in agony.

Beth followed the staffers to the edge of the cafeteria, begging Barlow to lower Matt's dosage. He ignored her. To be honest, it wouldn't have mattered at that point.

I'm no scientist, and to this day I'm not sure what exactly is in Newfutrisol. At a low dose, it robs you of your critical thinking, just enough to make you docile. Inject too much into a person, though, and they go completely insane, as Matt did.

That, at least, explains the personality breakdown, the madness, the cannibalism. What I still don't understand is how the physical symptoms – the rot and decay – began, nor how the infection could be spread by bite.

The next few days weren't all bad, I guess.

Mark succumbed quicker than Matt had, and was a gibbering maniac by the end of day three. It took a while for the staff to realize what was going on. At breakfast that day, Mark took a snap at Beth, and she punched him. Barlow broke it up and had them both shoved into a holding cell – together. When they were released, Beth's left arm was sporting teeth marks.

Beth seemed in strangely good spirits about the whole affair; when she finally re-emerged, she winked at me.

I wish I could describe the thrill of seeing the newly-zombified Mark Lobotomy pounce on Barlow, snap his neck and gnaw on his flesh while his body twitched and twitched. Or the glorious moment when the female staffer, ducking into an elevator to get away from Mark, found herself face-to-face with zombie Beth. By the time she comprehended what she had just walked into, the elevator doors were closing and Beth had her pinned to the back wall. I saw Beth sink her teeth into the woman's jugular, sending geysers of blood spurting up. The woman locked eyes with me, and then the doors shut for good.

The best, of course, was Parrish's demise. Once he realized what was going on, he tried to flee by car but crashed into a tree and wound up pinned underneath the wreckage. He'd regained consciousness by the time Mark and Beth found him, and was conscious for several more hours as the two of them tore him to shreds and devoured him piece-by-piece.

After that, though, the fun was over, as the zombies turned on me.

I managed to avoid my fellow inmates for a few weeks before Beth and Mark caught up with me. I found it odd that they had teamed up so effectively, given how deeply they'd hated each other in life; however, I didn't have long to ponder this fact before Mark's teeth were buried in my right forearm.

In a burst of frantic agony, I jerked my arm away, leaving Mark with a hunk of my flesh dangling from his jaws. This prompted Beth (evidently still harboring some vestigial hatred of Marcus) to turn on him, knocking him down and pinning him to the floor in order to claim the bite-sized chunk of me. She was too busy trying to wrench his jaws open to notice as I ran in the other direction.

Finding refuge in a supply closet, I tried the old movie trick of sawing off the affected arm before the infection could sink in. The crude operation worked, at least to an extent; while I've got some of the physical symptoms, I never really lost my mind like the others.

Of course, that may change. I'm already beginning to feel the affects of decomposition – I reek, my toes are beginning to rot off the bone, and I assume my brain will eventually start to decay. I don't know how long I have left, but I'm perfectly content to use my last few months continuing Parrish's work.

The Center's coffers are still pretty full. Say what you want about Parrish, he knew how to milk concerned parents out of significant coin. And now with the cost-cutting measures I've implemented, we should be able to keep the lights on as long as I'm still alive and twitching.

Of course, I do more than keep the lights on. I've made sure to keep our promotional efforts going, to ensure a steady supply of new punks arrive here every week and get treated with Newfutrisol – at a dosage just high enough to re-make them, but low enough that the kids don't start showing symptoms until they're back home with their respectable families.

You know, part of me thinks my parents would be proud of me for managing such a large-scale operation. Before I came here, I was a fry cook at Burger King. Now, I'm a new man.

I guess you could say the Parrish Center really straightened me out.

THE BALLAD OF HANK XXX

BY DAVID W. BARBEE

The very first Hank Williams was a pioneer of country western artistry, a treasure of the traditional American spirit, and a musical icon. The second Hank Williams revolutionized the country music genre into an audacious vision of beer swilling, tailgating, and hollow cowboy symbolism.

What a douche.

Luckily, the third Hank Williams came along. Breaking away from the long shadow of Bocephus, Hank III taught the dying country genre what it meant to be a true rebel. He was unwilling to fit into the box Nashville had built for his family, and struck out on his own to form various punk and metal bands.

And by his example, more Hanks followed.

Each one greater than the last.

Each one punker than the last.

The line of Hank Williams outlived country music itself. With the powerful charisma of the Hank Williams dynasty, humanity could finally embrace a glorious future of no-guts-no-glory punk rock righteousness. Punk overpowered all cultures and religions until all men and women were united in purpose and equal as fuck

And at the helm of this punk world order there was always a Hank Williams, for written in his very DNA was a deep adoration for music and rebellion. He was the godhead upon which the future was formed.

Hank III was the template. The measuring stick by which all his descendants measured themselves. His own son, Hank IV, would help storm the beaches of Jamaica in the great Weed Wars. The following Hank would apply his scientific genius to curing disease. Hank VIII was the first punk rock President, so popular that no intelligent politician would ever again run for office without some variation of his trademark mohawk.

Hank XV was queer as an eleven-dollar bill. He and his husband adopted a small army of refugee children during their diplomatic campaign to establish world peace. Thanks to his efforts, the global community would end all wars, live in harmony with the environment, and form a new religion known as The Church of Punk as Hell.

But for all his accomplishments, the world would always need a Hank Williams. It was a humanitarian imperative. So Hank XV donated a genetic sample and through a surrogate there came Hank XVI, who, at the age of three, became the first Pope of The Church of Punk as Hell. He spent half his life walking the earth, busking for spare change, doing good deeds, and hunting down the last Nazi punks until they were driven into extinction.

General Hank XIX expanded the Earth government's territory across the solar system. Though he never returned from his excursion across the Milky Way.

There followed an age of colonization. Punks were flung from Earth to distant moons and planets, establishing footholds for the Church. Within a century there was strife. Spread across the stars, the punks evolved into different breeds that feuded and warred. The lazy crust punks formed an army to resist the political rantings of the anarcho-punks. The skater punks bought into fascism and the vegan punks began performing human sacrifices.

Rivers of blood spilled across the stars, and the line of Hank Williams presided over it all. The twin Hanks XXIII found themselves on opposite sides, and eventually agreed to a duel to decide the fate of the solar system. The winner of the duel would finally claim sole ownership of their name while also winning the war for his side. Mankind watched as two Hank Williamses fought with chainsaws and killed one another simultaneously.

Nobody won the war and neither twin had an heir, so the mantle of Hank XXIV went to an unexpected candidate.

Of all the wiseass uncles, rowdy cousins, and distant not-worth-a-damn nephews, the next heir to the name was a third-removed niece of one of the twins' half-sisters. Her name was Henrietta Louise Annie Oakley McMeanmug, and she was sexy as hell with a shaved head. But with the wounds of war still fresh, many punks rejected her. A girl couldn't be Hank Williams. That was just stupid.

Still she persisted. She moshed and thrashed and toured every moon and asteroid. She ate the crowds' hatred and bathed in their spit. Some scholars would conclude that Hank XXIV truly was one of the most punk motherfuckers ever to live. But by a vast margin her reign would be seen as the moment that humanity, and therefore, punk rock, began its downfall.

Her son became the next Hank Williams. He spent all his time skateboarding and never even made it to the pros. The one after him was a great musician but couldn't fight for shit. The one after him could fight like hell but couldn't play a lick.

Faith in the Church of Punk as Hell waned. The punk community fractured like never before, and when all hope seemed lost, suddenly Hank XXIX choked on his latte and died.

By now, the bloodline had been diluted so that no one expected the next Hank Williams to embody true Hankness. But the scruffy teenager chosen for the mantle surprised them all. Unlike his uncles, Hank XXX could sing, play, fight, fuck, drink, smoke, and snort better than any punk ass motherfucker who stepped to him. He stood out from the other twenty-fifth century Hanks, though he had much in common with granny Henrietta. He was the only one in the universe who liked her, which to him was his surest proof that he was the realest rebel of them all.

It was the year 2474, and depending on who's telling the story, Hank XXX either saved or doomed the entire human race.

Punker Airlines had reserved every seat for him, but Hank XXX rode down in the cargo hold with the rigging. One of his eyes had been upgraded with a glass viewer orb, and his cheek still bore a wrinkled scar from when his concert on Phobos was bombed by anarchists. His mohawk had been woven into tight dreadlocks and he was covered in tattoos of cartoon characters, but with all that by the wayside he was the spitting image of the original Hank Williams.

As the roadies and hangers-on partied up on the main deck, Hank XXX perched on a stack of steel trusses and stared out a porthole at the stars. The void was littered with shattered satellites and junked spaceships, and as the debris floated by, a peninsula-sized statue of his own face captured his attention.

Monuments drifted throughout the solar system, most of them dedicated to the original Hank Williams or the holy Hank III. But these days the Church of Punk as Hell had already lost half its followers. Punk itself was split into dozens of splinter groups, each one professing to be punker than the last. Hank XXX had to admit that he preferred it that way. Hell, he was lucky only a third of mankind worshipped him instead of the whole shebang. He'd have been happiest if nobody believed in him at all. He hated being a celebrity, hated being placed on a pedestal for no other reason than his heritage. It made him a cog in a media machine that crossed the stars. He played his gigs and entertained his crowds, but he wasn't just an entertainer. They'd made him into an idol.

Half the crowds wanted to be rebels just like him and the other half wanted to rebel against him. To them he was a symbol of the entire herd of humanity, and all he really wanted was to just pick his fucking guitar.

But they forced him to be a savior. Even this next gig was part of the Church of Punk as Hell's plans. Hank XXX's manager had worked out a concert on the Moon that they all hoped would bring the rebel tribes back into the fold. And the lunar punks hated Hank Williams more than anyone else.

The Moon was the first celestial body to be colonized. Centuries later its facilities were long out of date and falling into disrepair, making it the solar system's ghetto. Its residents got by making art out of moon rocks and priding themselves on being the hardest of hardcore. The lunar punks saw the line of Hank Williams as decadent sellouts, and Hank XXX as a pampered pretty boy without a badass bone in his body.

Supposedly the fate of humanity rested on Hank XXX impressing the lunar punks with his show and thus ushering his people into a new age of punk unity. He didn't really believe it would happen like that, but a gig was a gig.

Hank's ship closed in on the Moon's pockmarked surface and landed on a concrete pad outside a gigantic glass dome showing hundreds of hairline cracks. The airlocks attached themselves and the roadies entered the cargo hold to unload the gear. Hank XXX hopped down from his perch and headed into the facility, dragging a wheeled luggage case behind him.

His manager, a stiff suit even without all the robot parts, led him deep into the space station's corridors. The place was a dump. The steel panel walls had warped and popped most of their screws so that sections of it bowed outward. The ceiling panels were stripped, exposing mazes of wires and conduits. The floor was as dirty as any street, caked in grime and sprinkled with trash. Mounds of gray moon dust were piled up in every corner.

Lunar punks roamed the halls, tall and scrawny and coated in gray. They watched the roadies and smoked homemade cigarettes. They sneered at Hank XXX as he passed by. His face was shrouded by his dreadlocks, but his luggage made him look like a tourist. They made their defiance known, but no one dared call out to him. They'd seen the video recordings of what Hank XXX did to hecklers.

"They'll come around when you start playing," the manager said in his toaster oven voice. He opened the door to Hank XXX's dressing room and let him inside, then hurried off somewhere.

The dressing room was once a janitor's closet, big enough to hold industrial cleaning equipment and a line of basin sinks. The walls were gray steel panels with various hazard signs bolted on. Stains covered everything, including the ragged loveseats that crowded the place at odd angles. Hank XXX locked the door behind him. His entourage would find him eventually, and he needed some privacy now that his face was slipping.

He approached a small mirror mounted to the steel wall and hauled his luggage case into one of the sinks. Unzipping the top, he revealed a shiny steel canister with a touch pad on the side. Hank XXX tapped in the security code and the top of the canister hinged upward. Inside, stacked atop one another on trays of wire netting, were faces. Each one was his, with the same burn scar on the left cheek from the show on Phobos.

Ever since the experiment, Hank XXX needed extra faces. The rest of his body held up fine, but sometimes his face would slide off his skull. It was a curse, but one he'd signed up for willingly. Even with the inconvenience of having to clone new faces and carry them around, he didn't regret the decision. He believed you could only regret something if you didn't really understand why you were doing it in the first place.

Hank XXX had undergone the experiment because he thought it would help destroy his fame. Celebrity wasn't the antithesis of punk, as the lunar punks believed. Celebrity was the antithesis of freedom. He only wanted to play his music, but Hank XXX carried the responsibilities of a political, social, and religious leader. He was constricted by his obligations to mankind itself. The burden turned him bitter, and eventually he decided that if he was going to be a god to them, he should get to be a god for real. Once the punk populace saw just how far into the heavens his pedestal reached, they'd surely reject him.

He had sought out the help of a celebrity warlock who lived out on Neptune. He was a new age shaman solving high society's biggest problems, bestowing wisdom and beauty while keeping everyone's precious integrity intact. He could even grant the galaxy's messiah actual messianic powers. Hank XXX's plan had been to give the people everything they'd spent the last five hundred years hoping for, because once they had it, only then would they realize what bullshit it was.

The warlock agreed to help, but he explained that the name Hank Williams was worshipped by so many that he already possessed vast powers. To achieve more, he would have to cross an enormous spiritual gulf. Hank XXX was already so close to a god that there was only one thing he could do: die. The defiance of death was the hallmark of any god, and the only triumph that escaped the long line of Hanks. Over the centuries they had worked miracles and saved mankind from destruction. They had bathed in the adulation of the masses, and the only step left to take was toward immortality itself.

The warlock revealed powders, incense, and a dusty tome of morbid chants. The incense would burn, the powder would be imbibed, and the chants would push him past the veil of death. Hank XXX snorted the powder without question, and he emerged from the ceremony as a member of the undead.

He found that there wasn't much difference to it, except for his face. Maybe it was because he looked so much like the original Hank Williams, but every few days the underside of his face would begin to rot and fester. The blood would turn to black jelly and the skin would dry out and pucker. He had to peel the face off and replace it with another. Luckily, getting flesh masks of his own face was easy.

The real problem turned out to be timing. Hank XXX hadn't found the right moment to reveal his new condition, and he refused to do it until the moment was right. His manager probably suspected something was up, but he was too busy booking the gigs and keeping the show on the road.

Now, Hank XXX reached up to his hairline and started to peel off his face when the door exploded inward. It was his manager, screaming like a busted microwave. "We gotta start the show! They're gonna tear the place apart if you don't get up there right now!"

Hank XXX didn't get a word out before his entourage filled the room. A pair of roadies took him by the arms and yanked him away from the mirror. Out in the corridor, the lunar punks were running back and forth, throwing dust balls that exploded into gray mist. The roadies covered their boss as best they could, elbowing scrawny punks out of the way and delivering Hank XXX up to the stage.

Beneath the cracked dome of glass, thousands of dusty gray lunar punks bounced off one another in a sea of thrashing bodies. Beer bottles flew back and forth across the arena. Shouts and screams echoed off the glass. Hank XXX saw a few people get murdered in front of the stage. His bandmates took their positions and someone put his guitar in his hands. When the lunar punks realized that the show was beginning, they gnashed their teeth at the stage, cursing Hank Williams' name.

Hank XXX looked back behind the curtains to see his manager giving him a robotic smile and two thumbs up. He knew there was no hope of uniting these punks with the rest of the human race, but a show was a show, so Hank XXX stepped up to the mic.

"Aight, I wanna see that fuckin' pit open up," he drawled.

The band laid into one of his early hits, "Jupiter's Bitch Tits," before running through "Starjob," "Hell Thruster," and "Hot Pussy Nightmare Town."

The next song was "Graveyard Spaceship," a nineteen-minute epic of thrashing guitars with five sets of garbage can drums. The crowd settled into the groove, moshing back and forth with the beat. But it all went to hell when his face began to peel on its own. During the third guitar solo, Hank XXX's forehead flapped down over his eyes. He kept playing, because he was a fucking professional, but this wasn't how he wanted to reveal his condition to the world.

He heard them laughing as his brow drooped down. Then his rotten nose broke free and the rest of his face dropped, dangling at the end of his chin. His bare eye sockets could see the lunar punks, and to his surprise they were smiling. The moshing stopped and the crowd rushed to the stage, gazing up at Hank XXX's exposed skull belting out his song. The strip of decomposed flesh swung back and forth as his jawbone bobbed up and down as he screamed the chorus.

Finally, the flesh mask dropped from his chin and was caught on the face of his guitar, where his frantic playing shredded it against the strings. Flecks of dead flesh and black blood sprayed out from Hank XXX's guitar, bathing the lunar punks in finely sliced gore.

They loved it.

The lunar punks opened their mouths wide to swallow bits of his flesh. They smeared it on themselves and each other, until his essence had spread across the entire arena. Hank XXX, his face laid bare to the bone, kept playing. The rest of his band abandoned their instruments and gathered around their leader. They called out to him, but he kept playing. They watched the skull face scream out more songs until they grew disgusted and retreated backstage.

When he finished his last song, the dusty gray faces in the crowd had grown rotten and black. Hank XXX smashed his guitar and ran away. He made it to his dressing room and got a good look at himself in the mirror. He gazed at the bare skull and listened as the entire moon base shook with the lunar punks' voices. They were chanting his name.

His manager rushed into the room. "Dude," he said in his toaster oven voice, "they're all turning into zombies! And they fuckin' love you! This zombie thing is spreading through the base like wildfire, man. You know what, I bet if it spreads across the system, then all the punks will unite again! I told you this show would be a fuckin' success!"

Hank XXX stopped listening. He was more famous than ever, universally adored. He'd never be free of the spotlight. He stared at the canister holding all of his cloned faces. Disgusted with himself, he started eating them.

EAT THE RICH

BY CARMILLA VOIEZ

Sally's call sounded desperate and confused. I peddled as quickly as I could to the crumbling multi-story car park. It was deserted, as usual. Not a tourist hot spot. If cars didn't get damaged by falling chunks of concrete they would be stripped of their tires within an hour of parking. I was surprised it hadn't been gentrified like the rest of the city, but no doubt that was someone's plan for the future.

They were on the basement level. Hazmat's gallery. More talented than Banksy but as yet undiscovered. As always I felt awe when I saw his work. A new piece had been started. A Doctor Marten boot kicking something that looked like a pig's head in a riot helmet. The blood spray looked particularly realistic.

Sally and Hazmat, my best friends and comrades. They accepted my weirdness and I loved them for it. Sally had a sort of post-punk Goth look with half her head shaven, and the other half a jungle of backcombed black hair set off by her Cleopatra-style kohl-smudged eyes. Hazmat was more your original 70s punk – green mohawk and black leather jacket. And me? I guess I was hard to explain.

Sally knelt beside Hazmat, pressing a cotton dressing against his cheek. She glanced up at me and tried to focus her eyes.

"It's me," I assured her.

"He's in a bad shape, Grinch," Sally answered. Her pierced lips curling into a worried smile.

"What happened?"

Hazmat tilted a bottle of cider against his lips. "They're in worse shape," he claimed proudly, nodding towards his crumpled sleeping bag.

I spotted three skinheads beneath the filthy, once-red, nylon bedding. Their necks and arms covered in vile fascist tattoos, deep blood-encrusted caverns in their racist skulls. "Fucking Nazis."

"They attacked him while he was painting," Sally said. "He did that with his sodding paint can."

"Did they cut his face?" I asked.

"Bit it," Hazmat said. "Fucking animals."

Animals? Nah. Humans were much worse. Especially the fasch.

"He should go to hospital, but he won't. I've given him some meds and I'll get some more. He can't stay here though. He needs somewhere cleaner."

"My couch is a bit cleaner, I guess," I said.

"It's cleaner than mine," she agreed. "Let's take him there. What about them?"

"We'll tidy up then set fire to the bodies. No one gives a fuck about a few dead Nazis. It's a bloody public service disposing of them," I said, meaning every word. "Love your new mural, Haz. The blood looks very real."

"It's theirs." His head bobbed forward. Cider and whatever drugs Sally had administered must have been working their magic on him. Immobile spikes of jade green crowned his exhausted head. *My fucking hero.*

I thought he was going to die. It seemed wrong not to take him to hospital even though he forbade it. Sally made sure he had the right antibiotics and pain relief, probably stronger than he would have got at Newham General. Who'd have known drug dealers made such great doctors? He was hallucinating and sweating profusely for thirty-six hours before his fever broke. When it did he looked older, thinner and impossibly pale.

"Nah, he's alright," Sally said. "I know people who would die for a pallor like that."

I snorted. "How are you feeling, Haz?"

"Like a fucking zombie," he said.

"You just need to eat something," Sally told him. "I'll grab some chips."

"Reckon I need some meat," he said.

I felt like I might vomit. "No meat," I told him. "Not in my house, you asshole." *Love would only permit so much. Eating animals under my roof? Not fucking likely.*

Sally seemed more sympathetic. "Maybe it's an iron deficiency. I'll see what I can get."

"Okay, but no meat. I mean it."

"I know you do, Grinchy poo. I solemnly promise never to bring the carcasses of slaughtered animals into your home."

Grinchy poo? I let it go. She was one of a tiny number of people I didn't want to punch. Since I'd been taking the T that had become a rare thing indeed. A fact that should probably have worried me more than it did.

She brought him dark green salad leaves and beetroot but he spat out the first and only mouthful.

He shook his head. "Fuck. I can't do it. Some thing's wrong with me. It's more than hunger. I dreamed terrible things. I dreamed of cracking skulls and shoveling down their contents. Sal, this bloody bandage itches. Can I take it off?"

"Let me look," Sally said. She peeled back the cotton gently then gasped.

"What is it?" Hazmat and I said in unison.

She didn't speak so I took a look.

"Bollocks!"

"What?" Hazmat asked. "What is it? Is it bad? Is it infected?"

"It's healed," I whispered. "Surely that can't be possible."

Sally shook her head.

He shrugged. "I feel really restless. I need to get out of here. I want a fight and I'd rather it weren't with you, Grinch."

"I'm sure I could take you anyway."

He laughed.

"A bunch of us are sabotaging a hunt this afternoon. I was

gonna bail, with you so sick and all, but if you're feeling better ... Plenty of rich wankers to punch while we wait for the next Nazi to come along. Direct your anger where it counts."

Hazmat grinned. His eyes shone in a way that would give me nightmares.

———

They were there with rifles, dogs and horses, the arrogant bastards. We shouted, threatened and generally got in the way. It was an impasse and it frustrated the hell out of the hunters. They were used to getting their way, and looked like they'd be happy to shoot us all – punks, anarchists and hippies alike.

Hazmat was bristling. It wasn't only the hair of his mohawk that stood on end. I could tell he wanted action. I felt just as excited. This was class war and animal rights activism rolled into one delicious bundle.

One of them felt brave enough to approach. We faced off, him with his rifle, us with our righteous anger. I felt Hazmat lurch beside me. I touched his arm, and he rewarded me with a deep scratch that drew blood. He pounced. I never imagined a human being could jump like that. The riding hat flew into the trees, and Haz dragged the rich bloke to the ground. His skull cracked open like an eggshell.

I couldn't see much of the attack as Hazmat's muscled torso blocked my view. It was only when he got up again, blood dripping from his mouth and covering his "Eat the Rich" t-shirt, that I saw the devastation. I vomited. Doubled over, I heard screams all around me. People fled. Dogs growled. Horses panicked and kicked out, dislodging their riders. The sound of bones crunching replaced the screams of terror and I fell unconscious.

———

I was back in my bedsit when I came to. Hazmat had showered and dressed in clean clothes. For a blissful moment I laughed at the vividness of my dream. Of course it hadn't been real. *Hazmat didn't just eat someone. Ridiculous.* This wasn't Hollywood, it was East London. My arm itched. I tried to scratch it but there was a bandage in the way.

"What's this?" I asked.

"Sorry, mate," Hazmat said, looking ashamed. "I think I scratched you. Sally patched you up, but it's a bit yellow and smells rotten. She asked me to give you some antibiotics when you woke up. I didn't tell her about what I did at the hunt. Do you think I should? Those toffs tasted so good, mate."

"You ate them? Bollocks. I thought … Shit!"

"And you wanted me meat-free. They were probably free range though, Grinch. And I only ate part of them."

"Which part?"

"Their brains … I'm a zombie aren't I? Diseased Nazi scum bites me and now I'm the living dead." Hazmat sniffed. "Well fuck it. I always said I wanted to eat the rich."

He handed me the pills.

"Does this mean I'll be like you?"

He shrugged. "I don't fuckin' know how it works, mate. Sorry though. It looks pretty deep. Are you in pain?"

I shook my head. "It just itches." I swallowed the pill.

"Like my face."

Thirty-six hours later, I was hungry for brains.

It sucked, but there were ways I could turn this to my advantage. I sprayed up my white quiff and pulled on my favorite striped jeans. I filled the pockets with as many coins as I could find around the bedsit. Admittedly it was no fortune, but all I needed was an in. Then I headed out, into the city.

You don't have to look for long in London to find those of our brethren without roofs over their heads. The great ignored. I'd often considered them a potentially unstoppable army come the revolution. My idea, if it worked, would just bring the revolution a lot closer.

The first poor bastard stank of piss. The ammonia hurt my nose, but out of respect I refused to show any signs of repulsion. I sat next to him on the shallow front step of a Georgian town house with twelve doorbells. He looked at my coolly.

"Are you a boy or a girl?" he asked.

Always the same question. "Neither," I answered. "But I could be your power animal. I can make you so strong you can take everything you need from those rich wankers who pass you by with their noses in the air."

"Are you some sort of pervert?"

I laughed. *Only as much as the next person,* I guessed. "Let me get you a coffee and you can listen while you warm your belly."

"You've got a deal. Don't skimp on the sugar though."

It didn't take as long as I expected to convince him. I suppose he had nothing left to lose and the thought of paying back in kind all the cops who had kicked or pushed him around sold him on my idea. I scratched his hand and left him with antibiotics. I would have preferred to gather my army in a large shelter, but that wasn't within my means. So I gave him the address of Hazmat's basement gallery and asked him to meet me there the following evening. As I walked away towards my next recruit, I hoped he'd survive the night.

It pained me to know what people would let me do in exchange for a hot beverage. Lack of shelter and regular food dehumanized people, and many of those I spoke to seemed to have lost all sense of self. Each day was just about survival to them, avoiding violence and eating the scraps they were given. This in a city where one-bedroom apartments sold for millions. It was obscene. I bought dozens of coffees and administered almost as many scratches. I could only bring myself to do it with their consent. It would be like pyramid selling, I reckoned. *First I scratch ten per day, then each recruit converts ten per day, and within a week we'll have over 20,000 super-strong zombie soldiers.*

After they turned, the zombies hung out together in the abandoned car park, getting increasingly hungry and frustrated. There were the inevitable casualties, but if I might be allowed to say it myself - it was fucking awesome. I made Hazmat very proud. An outcast army eager to wreak havoc and destruction. A nihilist's wet dream. In my mind we were simply soldiers in the class war and we would all be tested in battle the following evening.

Thousands of bodies swarmed together along city streets towards the palace, like one homogeneous mass with a hive mind. It was more than a mob. It was life.

Police in riot gear mobilized quickly and blocked the road ahead, twenty or more rows deep. They weren't taking our march lightly. I'm sure they intended to provoke the peasants into violence and arrest our asses. *Be careful what you wish for.* I felt no fear. I was indestructible. Hazmat and Sally on either side. No longer strictly vegan, but with a very specialized diet.

We were demanding our human right to food, shelter and dignity. It was immaterial that our dietary requirements were human brains. Beyond the armored pigs, great gates stood before Buckingham Palace, an ostentatious symbol of our oppression when we were still human. Once their riot helmets had been removed the police would be zombie food, followed by the Queen's guard. We would eat well this evening. We would climb the gates, supported by our comrades and swarm onto the property. *God save the fucking Queen, from us!*

The juddering of rubber bullets and live ammunition asked a question – how dare you come here? I could smell victory in the cranial fluids that washed down each mouthful of gray matter. I was dining on pork for the first time in over a decade. Blood lust rose inside me and I tore helmets, often with heads still attached, from the Metropolitan Police's shoulders. We bathed in a shower of gore, the zombie punks, the militarized homeless and the rest of the hooligans. *La Terreur* in Paris over 200 years before could not have tasted more sweet. The guillotine could not have been a more efficient executioner than our arms and teeth.

Hazmat grinned at me as he separated another cop from its helmet.

I grinned back then shrugged. "Hey guys. Tomorrow we're homeless. Tonight it's a blast!"

"Or we're living in a fucking palace," Sally whispered in my ear.

I was shoved with a riot shield and knocked into my friend. She fell backward, landing on her ass. I tried to reach for her. But she shook her head and laughed. "All good here," she shouted. "Carry on." She sprang to her feet and slammed forward like she was in a mosh pit. Fucking punks. I loved them all to bits. You couldn't keep them down. Alive or undead.

Armored vans, water cannons and SWAT teams descended on Green Park and St James Park as we munched through the riot police and clambered over the gates. Busbies, red jackets and bayonets charged at us. Some blades reaching their mark and felling us. Others aiming ineffectively at our chests. Behind us bullets whizzed through the air, hitting our backs and limbs. Water tried to knock us off our feet but made the Queen's soldiers fall on their asses instead. We descended on them like starving wolves, sating more than hunger as blood lust rose in each zombie.

My phone beeped. So did a hundred others. I fished into my jeans and pulled it out. Smeared blood across the screen. Emergency message. For their own safety, everyone must return to and stay in their homes until further notice. Was it just London on shut down or all over the country? I screamed with excitement. A stupid grin plastered across my face, I glanced around.

Those human comrades who were still alive looked afraid. This was no normal riot. I watched them flee, invariably ending up caught and loaded into police vans. I wondered whether anyone would believe the stories they'd tell. I wondered how many of us would survive this night. I wondered why I didn't care.

I had enough to care about. The hiss of skin tearing from muscle. The smell of blood and intestines. Hot viscera hitting my face. I closed powerful jaws around parietal bones and heard them crack as I exerted pressure. Blood hit my throat first then the spongy mush of cranial matter. A thousand electrical pulses shot around my head like a lightning ball and energy surged through neurons to every nerve ending making me shiver deliciously. I hooked fingernails under broken bits of skull to remove bone fragments and plunged my face into the makeshift bowls to dine. Over and over again. Each experience seemed new and unique, each taste sublime. I lost myself. My intellect fled and I forgot where I was. The doors gave way under our combined pressure and I darted through red and gold rooms. Between portraits and mirrors. Under arches full of skylights. I followed the scent of blood and human sweat, the sound of beating hearts. The gaudy gold and ugly paintings couldn't hold my attention. I only wanted to feed again.

I heard the rotary blades of a helicopter. Blindly I ran, tearing my way through drapes and paneled doors, relying on my senses of smell and hearing. Others moved with me. Although I couldn't recognize their faces in my rage, I knew they were of my kind and would not provide me with my next meal. The helicopter noise retreated. It was airborne. Presumably taking humans to safety. But some remained. I could smell them. Hear them whimper.

Smoke rushed into the room. It tasted like vinegar and made me screw up my face. I retreated from the open doors, past rows of chairs and toward a dais and the thrones. Boots hit the floor hard, echoing between walls. Plastic shields taller than me, pushed through the ornate archway and gathered to form a wall. Behind them insect-like gas masks and helmet mounted torches glared at me. I fled to a door on my right and out of the room, chased by the sound of dozens of rubber soles hitting marble. This room was filled with the slow rolling mist as well. I'd encountered it before. Last time it made my eyes burn, my nose run and my chest threaten to implode. This time it was just a nasty smell that overwhelmed all other scents. With my ears full of footsteps and my nose full of tear gas I had no idea where the whimpering humans were hiding. Other zombies ran blindly through the corridor, equally disorientated. I recognized Hazmat as he stumbled over to me. His right foot bent at a strange angle. I pulled his arm over my shoulders and hurried him along.

The palace was a warren of hundreds, perhaps thousands, of rooms. The mist had permeated all of them. It was time to get out. A security camera followed our movements as we lurched into a room I hoped would lead to an outer wall, but again the only windows were far above us. I was sick of this place, of the smell, of the sounds, and the gold shining everywhere. But we were so lost. More doors, more rooms, yellow this time and at last tapestry drapes on the far wall. Together Hazmat and I hit the window with an ornate chair that shattered into pieces as it hit the glass. I grabbed a candelabra and used it as a battering ram. The pane splintered and we took it in turns to kick at the weak spot until at last the window smashed and we climbed out.

There were soldiers here too. They pounded us with bullets as we ran to the wall. It was high, but I'd seen Hazmat leap and was sure he could make it. We threw ourselves at the unforgiving stone and clawed our way to the railings at the top. I looked back and saw piles of dead. Retreat and regroup, that was the plan. I hoped Sally would make it out.

Smoke filled the skyline and sirens wailed in every direction. The idea of fleeing for safety seemed ridiculous now. Instead we headed towards Downing Street. London was burning and we were hungry. It would be one hell of a barbecue.

THE ADVENT OF NOISE

BY LEO X. ROBERTSON

You've just broken up with Stephanie over the phone and are about to get on a direct flight to London for an annual conference on the tensile strength of vulcanized rubber, held in the Holiday Inn, where you will be staying. This gives you no time to see the city and country you'll be visiting for the very first time in your life. So, the only people you can sleep with are coworkers. Your newfound loneliness makes this a tragic inevitability, which has caused you to drink three beers already, though it isn't yet noon.

You sit in Newark Liberty International Airport's CBGB restaurant and don your headphones, plugging them into a new expensive iPod that she never would've let you buy. You've loaded it with Felix and the Ratdicks' seminal live recording, *Why is White Supremacy Still a Thing?* It's the only no-wave recording the band ever made, while they were all zombies on the run from The Taste Police: everything previous to *Supremacy* was punk.

You admire the apparently abstract artwork of the album cover until, dropping your fork into the Suicide Salad that accompanies your Sloppy Joey Ramone, you realize it depicts the moment the shotgun fired, its barrels pressed beneath Felix's chin, exploding his head like a meat-and-bone firework. Wow, you think, and now more emotion rushes to you while viewing this one simple image than could ever have hoped to reach you from, say, the lunch in front of you. Synapses light up with the chemical pleasure of noise and transport you to 70s NYC, soundwaves transcribing a story in your brain, the tale of the Ratdicks' resurrection, the birth of no-wave.

The Ratdicks argued over their music's aesthetic: the three chords that had inspired the band and provided their first fifty LPs seemed to be running dry, or so claimed lead guitarist Crispin. He spat in his hands, wiped them on his Mohawk and said, "Our music makes too much sense! We're becoming poseurs. I won't be in a band that stays where it is, stands on its mark, plays its instruments professionally. Punk is motion. No more of this intro and outro and verse and chorus bullshit: I want all middle! Make noise from beginning to end. Offer no explanation. I'll die for it if needs be."

After hearing this, a despondent Felix, lead singer of the Ratdicks, took his girlfriend Amber to the dingy Times Square burger place they loved. He took out his anger on her, had it spill out of him in the shape of one of his tedious tirades. As a familiar silence befell them, a screaming woman outside caught a stray bullet through the cheek that blasted a hole in the back of her skull, spraying the window in front of Felix with blood and sharp chips of bone, which cracked the glass. A shell made a cartoon *wheeoooww* sound as it dropped and smashed through The Paramount Building; bricks of it slammed into parked cars, their alarms instantly wailing; and the shockwave hit the window near Felix and ruptured it at the indentations where bone chips had taken their home.

Customers poured out the place, shouting and yelling and brazenly rolling over the shattered window's angry rows of glass teeth.

Outside were The Taste Police, the symbols of their flags pure nonsense to Felix and Amber, their aims, beyond chaos, as-yet unclear. A rifle pointed in Felix's direction and a policewoman fired. His vision slowed down as, devoid of emotion, he watched the bullet pierce Amber's back and run through his chest, right into his heart. A deafening *clack!* sounded out, like two steel balls slamming together, and he fell back into the mirrored night-world of the afterlife, onto its version of the entrance to Central Park's Ritz-Carlton, in front of a giant worm which said to him, "Crispin was right, man! Your music is stale."

"This shit again?" he said, scratching his balls.

The worm radiated the warmth of a loving hand pressed against a fevered forehead, its skin many skins from Felix's life, about one for each year he'd been alive, flattened and sewn together like the many interlaced birds of an Escher drawing. At the end of the worm was a hole, a space for a missing jigsaw puzzle piece that would prevent this sickly-looking being from leaking its many ornate inner organs. The worm needed the skin Felix was wearing.

"You have disconnected from yourself," the worm said. "Take me and return reborn."

Behind Felix were pyramids of human cubes, bright and fresh as whale meat, streaming gravity-painted watercolor art with the gallons of blood that drained from their structures and wound across bleached tiles, which stained for good. The Taste Police built them as a barbaric demonstration of exactly what they didn't want. Examining the materials the Police had used to make these structures, Felix picked up an awl, a bolo knife and a leather string. In desperation, he looked to the worm, to the world around him, and sighed, taking his jeans off, cutting a slit around the centre of his belly, stepping into the worm and screaming in agony as he sewed himself with the awl and leather into its open end. The worm shrank and hardened like a scorpion tail, using the energy of the water it lost to transport him back to the living realm.

Thrown out of an ambulance, Felix barreled into the crowd waiting outside CBGB, where the Ratdicks held a Sunday-night residency, frequented by Bowie, Springsteen and Basquiat— something Felix had been as quick to tell people as to add that he didn't care.

His fans cheered the sight of his diseased skin, which suppurated and ached. Muddy fanzines littered the streets outside, as did safety pins and buttons.

"Felix!" Crispin said, bursting out the front door. He suppurated, his mephitic stench arousing the fans at the front of the queue. The Taste Police had slaughtered him earlier today in the CBGB green room's pile of rat-bitten bedding where he took his Sunday afternoon naps, and he too had been reborn. "We're on in fifteen. They got you too, huh?"

Felix nodded and coughed up a sickly green phlegm, lungs rattling with injured wheezes. "They'll come here next and wipe everyone out!"

Here they came, The Taste Police, hounding NYC, murdering and recruiting, their primordial blob of members expanding and splitting into violent protrusions like the fingers of a fetus developing in the womb.

The Milk Twins, bass and drum player of the Ratdicks, ran to the club's entrance, playing nervously with their ruby-coated dreadlocks, their virginal goatsilk skirts sopping in the rust of almost-dried blood that coated the ground.

"The Taste Police? Not again!" Stacey Milk said, tugging up her fishnets, which acted now as an external mesh for her sloughing zombie skin, beleaguered by her death and reincarnation in Grand Central station where the Police had known to find her whoring.

"We'd better start performing straight away!" Helga Milk said, tightening her corset a half-inch too much and cleaving the skin of her abdomen in twain, sending herself scurrying back inside on fleshless legs, an integumentary train flapping at her heels as embarrassingly as toilet paper stuck on a high heel.

The Twins came back outside in makeshift pantyhose they'd sliced out of cymbal covers, carting Felix's new, demented and godless T-shaped vessel inside. On stage, in front of an eager audience of greasy freaks, they propped him on a stool and he shuffled about to sit properly, whereupon his tail expanded into a chitinous bass guitar, the likes of which he'd never played before. That was the key. Seeing this, Helga took to the mic, Stacy to lead guitar, and Crispin to drums. To create a new genre, they'd have to unlearn everything they thought they knew about music.

The band battered out what their hearts composed, and as they played, a wall of fuzz and crunch emerged from the enormous speakers behind, to Crispin's evident elation. He'd said he'd die for it if necessary, and destiny had duly rewarded the Ratdicks for their sacrifice!

Yes, a wall of sound, whose effect was not lyrical nor even sonic but physical, a continuous distorted onslaught that defied the logical progressions of other media and headed straight for visceral, palpating the very organs of the strung-out kids in front of them, pumping air out their lungs, piss out their kidneys, blood out their hearts. Women screamed in ecstasy at the sensation of low-frequency sounds, as if they were making love to subsonic ghosts, peaks and troughs shuddering through their genitals with overwhelming pleasure. But this was not a performance of previously defined human sensation; it evolved beyond base comprehension. It just *was*, and what it was propagated out of CBGB and blasted away The Taste Police's weaker ranks, the swarm of them decaying to only their strongest ten percent.

Felix would ordinarily attack the audience by this point, but the guitar distracted him, bashing and blistering his face. Beyond its flailing structure he saw Amber in the audience, in her leather jacket, face wiped of its typical snarl and instead looking as serene as the dead. Peels of flesh ran from her temples and made flaps of her cheeks. He tried to cry out her name, but the noise dissolved it, and had anyone in the audience heard it, it wouldn't have mattered, as they were now as detached, as zombified, as Felix himself.

The Police burst in and continued their job of taking out targets of their anarchic cleansing, ensuring the tasteless stayed in the afterlife. They grabbed Amber, and she tried to scream.

"You see that?" Felix mouthed to the band, who nodded.

Stacy slung the guitar on her back as they left the stage, and Helga thrust her mic at the speakers behind them to keep the audience entranced by a constant screech of feedback, a success in the books of these, the first connoisseurs of the incipient no-wave genre.

Outside screamed the dying siren of the upturned ambulance in which Felix had arrived, its rotating beacons flashing a violent red across the city's wretched streets. Its sound re-energized Felix's scorpion component, which thickened into a beetle-shaped club.

The gang saw Amber's glowing corpse in the back of a speeding military jeep, so Crispin got on his motorbike, as did the twins, who held each other by one arm as they stood on foot pegs on either side of the bike, hooking their arms around Felix, who sat at the back of the seat, in reverse, the venomous spine of his tail sticking into the asphalt. Witnesses reported the sparks that flew from the tail as appearing "as if Electricity herself had been angered for the last time."

The twins swung baseball bats into the faces of newly recruited police as the gang chased the glowing jeep to an ad hoc military base at the mouth of the Hudson, where the ur-policemen towered tall and lizard-like, their reptilian scales bursting through makeshift uniforms.

Felix's tail slithered and expanded as it formed dry inner chambers that hissed like a rattlesnake when he shook them. The gang crept forward, the twins swinging their bats into the policemen that approached. But it wasn't long before the ur-policemen assembled like a wall of scales by the harbor and rushed the crew, decapitating Crispin a second time today, the vertebra of his sloppy neck severing with greater ease than the last time. They smashed their reptilian fists into the stomachs of the twins, whose spines shot an impressive distance behind their slumping corpses. The policemen held Felix by both arms, secured his tail with their enormous fists and a man in a lime-green nylon suit, with a camera slung around his neck, approached and pressed the barrels of a shotgun beneath Felix's chin.

"Pull the trigger," the man said.

Amber's face caught the moonlight and glowed a green Felix had never seen before. Her fate was as sealed as his.

He tugged his fingers down on the trigger, and every hair on his body sprang out on command, his wavy locks unfurling and reaching out for the air's charge as if lightning was about to strike. He hadn't heard the shotgun's blast, so instantaneous was the annihilation of his head, but as his feet landed on asphalt beneath him, he knew he'd returned to the afterlife, whose approximation of the Brooklyn Bridge beneath him yielded to his immense gravitational pull such that the U in the centre where he stood became a V, an arrow tip for the tumbling policemen that rolled towards him from either side way above, morning light shining across their machetes and samurai flags, their cannons and their horses. So the policemen were killing themselves now too, in order to double-, triple- or quadruple-kill the victims that insisted on returning as newly emboldened zombies, to force them through several dimension-layers of death away from the world whose integrity of wholesomeness the police apparently cared so much about.

As a blade whipped past his ear, as bullets rifled in slow motion towards him, as the collective force of the armies' rumbling wobbled the bridge such that he was now floating, Felix called out the name of his salvation: "Amber."

A hot beam of light shot through the clouds from above and held Felix in his spotlight, carrying him upwards from the world around him, which froze. He rose up in the fresh, misty air of a morning's garden stroll. Below him, the bridge collapsed, the police moving at infinitesimal pace, lit up in shafts of crepuscular rays that shot a eulogy of light across their factions.

Felix rose with the bittersweet mix of gratitude and shame that accompanies an almost-too-late request for help, but consoling clouds drained of their color and released their slow, thick rain, becoming pure white as they brought Felix through them.

There, he saw her again. Since this morning, he'd been a dick to her, died, resurrected, invented a new music genre, died again, and now apologized. They would remain in this sacred pocket of Death One as exalted fugitives, safe in the knowledge that together they had helped to gift humanity with a new style of music, been there for the advent of noise.

Listening to the Ratdicks, you don't ask any questions of Felix, don't demand any sense from what you absorb. There is no Stephanie, no Newark Liberty International Airport, no Holiday Inn, no vulcanized rubber; there is only fuzz, distortion, texture, noise. You close your eyes and let the wall of sound hit you where you need to hurt or heal.

Opening your eyes again, you see Felix sitting opposite you with a curdled zombie grin, and he is there with you as you feel whatever this feeling is, now and always: for there is no beginning and no end; there is only all middle.

THE GOOD SAMARITANS

BY SAM REEVE

Three hours prior they had watched the small town of Kamsack, Saskatchewan, disappear in the rearview mirror, and were swiftly swallowed up by a horizon as wide and flat as anything they had ever seen. To their left, fields of hazy brown wheat undulated gently in the breeze, and to their right sunshine yellow fields of blooming canola rose gloriously from the black earth.

The Chevy Astro they drove had seen better days - one of its rear side windows was just a plastic bag duct taped over the hole. It flapped loudly in the window and became shredded, needing to be replaced every few hours. The front bumper, also held on with a zealous use of duct tape and guitar strings, would have made Red Green proud. The back bumper featured a silver Jesus fish with a mohawk and a fading Altar Boys sticker. On one side of the van, however, their band's logo was painted proudly in huge, shining letters. This was the one part of the van they kept in pristine condition. It read *John and the 3:16's.*

Heavily tattooed arm hung lazily out the window, over-sized Hawaiian shirt billowing around him, Rick's beard flew behind him like a scarf on a jogger. The guys liked to tease him, saying he looked liked Santa's reject son who lived in the Bahamas. "Dude, where are we?" he asked from the front passenger seat.

John, the driver, squinted and hunched his shoulders as he looked out ahead at the upcoming sign. Bullet holes riddled it to such a degree that he couldn't make out the destination, but he noted the little gas station symbol at the bottom.

"I don't know, but we can fill up in about 15 minutes. Maybe someone there can point us in the right direction, although I'm still pretty sure Estevan is along this highway, from what I remember of the map."

"I told you, save maps offline on your phone. Isn't that what I told you?" said Josh, who sat behind Rick. He ran his hands through his greasy dyed hair that had faded to a weird orange, like the color of a mattress stained from years of sweaty sleep.

John tightened his grip on the wheel. The previous night's show had been frustrating for them, with a poor turnout and even poorer pay. Their opener, a Christian hardcore band called The Catholixxx, had sworn so much during their set that most of the parents chaperoning their kids had dragged them away in disgust. He reminded himself why they played shows in church basements in crummy little towns, and glanced at the tattoos across his knuckles that matched the side of their van. *John 3:16*.

Isaiah snored in the back next to Josh, closed eyes hidden beneath thick curly bangs. His snakebite pierced mouth hung slack, drool threatening to escape down a chin that couldn't yet grow facial hair. Rick was always sure to point this out when Isaiah poked fun at his voluptuous beard.

Josh nudged Isaiah awake, and he peered, bleary-eyed, out the window at the passing prairie landscape. "Where are we?" he groaned.

"Lord, have mercy," John sighed, shaking his head and perking up in relief as the gas station appeared in the distance, shimmering in the July heat.

They pulled up next to the pump, and all of them jumped out except for Isaiah, who took it as an opportunity to go back to sleep. The gas station's signs were rusted, the paint peeled. Rick went inside to look for the attendant, while John and Josh went to try pumping the gas. It was an older pump, the kind that needed to be paid for in cash.

A minute later, Rick came out, shaking his head.

"No one's here," he said.

"What?" John said, in disbelief. "Must be out back smoking or something. Is there a back office?"

"Why's it unlocked is what I really want to know."

John entered the gas station, looked around. It smelled strange, musty, but there was also something else, something he couldn't quite put his finger on. He peered over the counter, stuck his head into the back room. Nothing. Looking back out through the scratched glass of the door at their van, he let out another long sigh, and threw down a couple twenties by the cash register. They couldn't afford to wait around for some attendant who couldn't be bothered to even be there. John and the 3:16's had to rock for the crowds at the Estevan Alliance Church in five hours! They were opening for their pals Socks and Sandalwood from Winnipeg, who had played with them during their infamous first show where the church stage had collapsed and the preacher refused to pay them when he saw that some of them bore the "mark of Cain".

About 10 km from the gas station something appeared up ahead, a change in scenery from the fields and endless sky.

"What the..." Rick trailed off, eyes going wide when they neared enough to see it was a person shuffling along in the middle of the road.

John stopped the van abruptly, jolting everyone to attention. "What the heck dude!?" said Isaiah, fully awake and alert.

The man in the road walked slowly, limping a bit, dragging his right leg like he had a broken ankle. His plaid button up shirt blew out behind him in the breeze, revealing his stained undershirt. It was difficult to tell from behind, but the man appeared quite old, his skin covered in liver spots...or maybe they were welts?

"He's walking weird," said Isaiah.

John gripped the steering wheel a little harder, biting his lower lip.

"What should we do?" asked Rick

. "What do you mean, 'what should we do'? He's obviously in

need of help," said John. He pulled the car up to the man's right, rolled down the window. "Hey, sir, you ok? It's awful hot out here."

The man turned, and they all stared. His eyes were a strange yellow shade, like some kind of animal. A bit of blood trickled down his nose, and he didn't react when John spoke to him other than turning towards them. His nostrils flared slightly, but he didn't seem to hear him, or understand him, at least.

"This isn't right," said Rick.

"No shit," said Josh. "Maybe he doesn't speak English?"

Isaiah rolled down his window a crack. "*Parlez-vous Anglais*?"

"Why would a French dude be out here, dumb ass?" said Josh.

"Hey, screw you. Give me a break."

"Language!" said John, who rolled down his window all the way. He leaned out to wave at the stranger, who stood still, staring at them and making sniffling sounds. He cocked his head to the side, his wild eyes suddenly noticing the outstretched hand.

"What the heck…" Josh trailed off, leaning over Isaiah to get a better look at the guy. "This is so not right. What's wrong with him?"

"Maybe he's a hitchhiker who got in an accident?" Isaiah shrugged.

"We gotta take him to a hospital," said John resolutely. They all turned to look at him, jaws dropped.

"No *bleeping* way!" said Rick, mocking John with his tone. "He doesn't look...stable."

"Are you kidding me right now? I know you've read the book of Luke, dude. We can't leave this guy out here. He can barely walk, he's no threat."

"What if he pukes in here? You wanna smell that all the way to Estevan?" countered Josh.

"John's right though," said Isaiah. He pointed to the WWJD patch sewn onto his pants with dental floss. "He needs our help."

John nodded to them and opened his door, slowly, despite Rick and Josh's continued protests. The stranger still stood there, silently wobbling. His eyes darted to John, who approached him with open arms. "It's ok, don't worry. We're here to help, sir. Why don't you come with us? We can take you to a hospital."

The man still said nothing, but let John place a hand on his shoulder and gently guide him towards the van. Isaiah opened the side door and moved to the middle seat.

"Oh no way, I don't want him in the back here," said Josh, a look of disgust smeared across his face. "Jesus never said anything about picking up weird hitchhikers with diseases."

"Quiet," said John as he pointed to the empty seat and pushed the man down into it. "Jesus never had a van and probably hitchhiking wasn't even a thing back then...and he definitely chilled with a lot of lepers, so deal with it"

"You got us there..." Rick admitted, under his breath.

The man sat, sniffed the air and cocked his head to one side. John got back into the driver's seat and started the van, continuing down the way they had been headed. "I'm pretty sure if we keep following this road we're gonna be in Estevan, or at least some other town. Keep checking your phones for service."

The guys all pulled out their phones, holding them up to check for the illusive bars. Still nothing. Josh pinched his nose at the stench of the man, and it was an accomplishment to gross him out. Their hitcher began to gnash his teeth a little, made slurping sounds. Isaiah gagged a little but tried keeping a straight face as best he could.

"It's gonna be ok, sir," said John, looking at the man in the rearview mirror. "We're good guys. We're just taking you to get help." Not ten minutes after they had picked the guy up they saw buildings glinting in the distance, signaling civilization. As they neared, John turned to the back to reassure them. "See? This all going to work out."

As John finished his sentence and smiled to himself, feeling in his heart that God would be looking down on their little punk band favorably for their good deed, the mysterious stranger turned to Isaiah with unexpected speed and bit into his neck.

Isaiah screamed, blood gurgling from his mouth. They all shouted and the van swerved in the road, threatening to go into the ditch. John slammed on the brakes, the man flew sideways, and briefly let go of Isaiah, who fought to get away but was stuck in his seat belt. He held his hand to his neck, a red mess of veins and ripped flesh. His eyes wide, mouth moving but no words coming out. Blood sprayed all over Josh, who looked on in horror as they all screamed and scrambled to exit the vehicle.

Quickly, the man turned back to Isaiah. Josh unbuckled his seatbelt but was stuck between the monstrous stranger and the only door in the back of the van. He turned his head, looking for a way out. The instruments and amps crowded the back to a degree that he couldn't climb over them, so he went out the only way he could. He pushed through the thin plastic bag that covered the missing side window, emerging from the hell inside like a baby ripping through placenta. Just as he had almost cleared the van, the vicious stranger grabbed hold of his ankle and bit down hard. Kicking back with his other foot, Josh broke the man's grip.

John and Rick had already jumped out and were running down the highway toward the little town. Josh fell onto the pavement, bashing his head, but got up and limped after them. It wasn't until they were about a hundred yards away that they stopped to catch their breath and look back at the van, which sat sideways in the middle of the road, doors open. It shook slightly from the feast that took place within.

"What the fuck was that?" said Josh, panting. Blood trickled down his head from where he'd hit the road, and his ankle wound had already soaked his entire sock and shoe red. "And why the fuck did you leave me in there!?"

"Sorry, seriously, just…" Rick said, still in shock.

"I don't know who he was, but we need to go. That guy could come after us.," said John. He looked behind them at the town. Probably a 20-minute walk, tops.

"But Isaiah…" even as Rick said his name, he knew it was futile.

"He's rockin' out with the good Lord above," muttered John, who started walking towards the town. They kept a watchful eye behind them as they went, worried the man would creep up on them.

The town's welcome sign was also shot to shit like the one they had seen earlier. It certainly wasn't Estevan, merely some nameless village with a few houses, a couple abandoned-looking businesses, and a small church, its steeple rising above everything else.

"Hello!?" Rick called out, and walked over to the first house they reached. He knocked on the door, but no one answered. A few cars were parked along the side streets, but they saw no people. "Shit."

"It's fine," said John. "Everyone's out working, you know? We just gotta head somewhere safe, make a phone call."

"I don't feel so good," said Josh, wobbling on his feet. His ankle was swollen, the skin discolored all the way up his shorts. He stumbled and fell, saying no more.

Rick scooped him up by the shoulders, and John took his ankles. They carried him to a small general store that doubled as a post office. They called out as they crashed through the front door.

A woman in jean overalls stood behind the counter, her back to them. They put Josh down, and John stepped up to her. "Hey, we really need some help, where's your phone?"

"Ma'am, where are we?" asked Rick.

The woman swayed a bit, then slowly turned to them. Her eyes yellow like the man who'd attacked them. Well, her left eye - the right one was missing, just a scabby socket where it used to be. They screamed, tried picking up Josh, but dropped him when she bounded over the counter.

Rick fell back, knocking over a spinning greeting card display rack. The woman got tangled in it, briefly, but it gave John enough time to notice the mop leaning against one of the shelves just behind them. He grabbed it, shoving the mop end in her face. "Back! We're just trying to use your phone!"

Coming to his senses, Rick scrambled up and pulled Josh by the shoulders to the back of the store. The woman waved her arms, confused by the mop. She gnashed her teeth like the other man had, trying to claw her way towards them.

At the end of his rope, John pulled the mop back and smashed the woman in the face with it. "Lord forgive me!" he said, taking a second swing at her. This time it knocked her down, and hit her head on the edge of the counter before crumpling onto the floor. Dark blood, almost black, oozed a bit from the crack in her forehead.

John and Rick both looked at each other, too shocked for words. The bell on top of the door jangled, and they turned to the front of the store. Another man, or whatever he was, shuffled quickly towards them. Unable to lift his leg high enough to get over the fallen woman, he tumbled down on top of her.

They grabbed Josh and dragged him through the emergency exit at the back. It led to a small side street, and across from them was a patch of grass and a swing set. They stopped once there and looked around.

Down the street were two other figures. In the other direction, a half dozen people were heading towards them.

"Oh crap!" said John. He looked around, hoping for an answer, an escape. He saw the steeple and knew where to go. "Come on," he said, hoisting Josh up and over his shoulders with a strength he didn't know he possessed. "This way."

As they crossed the church's neglected lawn, dotted with blooming dandelions, they heard the crunching of footsteps to their right. A woman in a floral-print sundress headed towards them. Her gait was off, eyes yellow like the rest.

"How many of these people are there?!" said Rick.

They carried Josh up to the church as fast as they could, feeling a wave of relief that the doors were unlocked. John called out, " Hello? We need some help!"

They laid Josh down on the carpeted aisle between the pews. The church, probably built in the 40s or 50s, appeared to only have a couple small offices at the back, and some stairs leading to a basement. Rick returned from scouting out the place and threw his hands up in exasperation. "What do we do? Is he gonna be ok? This is so fucked!"

"Shoot, I was hoping for a kitchen, they'd have knives and towels then," said John. He frowned, thinking. "Also, watch your mouth. We're in His house now."

Rick shot him a stupid look. "Those people...things...are gonna come in here any minute, dude!"

"No," John said, shaking his head. "We're ok. They're...just possessed or something. They can't enter into God's house." He stood up, moved towards the door. As he was about to crack it open to peer out, a hand shoved the door open and reached for him. "Oh crap!"

John threw all his weight against the door, crunching the outstretched arm. It pulled back, and he held the door. "Quick," he shouted at Rick. "Get something to prop this closed. They're coming in!"

Rick looked around, but there wasn't anything big enough. He ran to the closest pew, but it was fixed to the floor and wouldn't budge. Same with the pulpit. "Uhhh...shit!" Rick looked back to John, exasperated.

"Hurry!"

Rick noticed the carved crucifix hanging above him. "Sorry Jesus," he said, knocking it down. It left an ugly gouge in the wall as it fell. He dragged it to the doors, and they propped it against them. "Are you sure this is heavy enough?"

John stood back to check. Either it was heavy enough or the freaks outside had stopped trying to get in. He pressed his ear to the door, but heard nothing.

Rick backed up into someone. "Hey, watch it," he said, going instantly white when he realized John was beside, not behind him. He turned. It was Josh. Eyes yellow, leg a swollen grey lump that oozed dark blood, he no longer appeared to be the Josh they knew and loved.

"Josh! Hey, you're ok!?" said John, hopeful.

Rick shook his head, knowing the truth. That's when the freaks on the other side of the door decided to make their second attempt to enter the church.

All hell broke loose. The door and the huge crucifix leaning against it were no match for a half dozen of those people, and it came falling down, nearly knocking RIck over. He caught it in time, and hoisted it up like a shield. Rick threw the crucifix at the people who'd stepped through the church doors, knocking them back into each other. Their collective stench made him nauseous, and as he turned tail to run for the pastor's office he nearly puked.

John held out his hands, trying to calm Josh, trying to reason with him even though his words fell on dead ears. John side-stepped his way in between the pews, followed by a lurching Josh and more attackers behind him. He ran up the left side of the church and joined Rick. Just before they could close the door behind them, Josh grabbed Rick's arm.

"Get the fuck off me!"

John grabbed the first thing he saw - an oversized Bible with gilded pages. He smashed Josh in the face with it. Teeth went flying. Bloody sludge poured from his nose. He fell back, enough for Rick to shut the door.

They pushed the pastor's desk up against it, which held. The attackers moaned, scraped their nails down the wood. John looked around, didn't see anything weapon-like. Rick looked down at the desk, and did find a pair of car keys next to a framed picture of the pastor and his wife.

"Hey, you think we could actually get out of this place?" he said, jingling them.

John's hands shook. A small window at the back of the office offered a glimpse into the backyard of the church. They couldn't see anyone out there, but they did see what they assumed was the pastor's old Lincoln parked next to a crab apple tree.

Gingerly lifting the Bible, John briefly ran his fingers over the embossed cross on its cover. "Let's do this," he said, and smashed the small window with it. Knocking free the remaining shards, he threw the good book out first, then stood on the chair to get a leg up over the sill.

John fell face down into the grass, followed quickly by Rick, whose Hawaiian shirt snagged on an errant piece of glass remaining on the window. A jagged scratch ran up his belly, but he ignored it, throwing the keys to John as they neared the Lincoln. Throwing the Bible in the back seat, they peeled off as some of the yellow-eyed locals hobbled around the corner of the church towards them.

―――――

Sideswiping a parked car as he drove them towards the outskirts of the little town, John slammed on the breaks just before they hit the highway. Someone stood in the road before them, blocking the way. It was the pastor, waving his hands at them. Blood soaked his plaid shirt and khaki pants. They couldn't see the color of his eyes from where they were.

"What do we -" Before Rick could finish, John slammed on the gas, hurtling towards the old man. The pastor doubled over and rolled up the hood, cracking the windshield before flying off to the right of them. Flecks of blood dotted the busted up wind-shield. They watched in the rearview mirror as the crumpled figure of the pastor slowly became nothing more than a small speck.

"Give me a fucking break," said John.

EARWORM

BY BRENDAN VIDITO

1. The Nameless Band

Damon woke in the still-dark hours of morning to find his latest one-night stand sitting up in bed, watching him. He lived above a laundromat in a run-down area of town, and the blinking sign outside threw a neon glow through the curtains, lighting up patches of her face and body. She was naked except for her thrift-store bomber jacket, and redolent of the beer and weed they'd shared the night before. Her chemical green hair was a wild tangle about her head, and a smear of black and purple eyeliner dragged down one cheek like the warning colors of a poisonous lizard. Her smile, however, was the most unnerving thing of all. Whenever she smiled—something she'd done frequently while they'd talked at the bar—it was usually a tight-lipped curl, but the one she wore now was manic, impossibly wide, her teeth crimson with neon blood.

"I just came back from the most amazing show," she said, the words whispered through clenched teeth.

"You had a dream," Damon replied, easing back into his

pillow after she'd startled him into an upright position. "Go back to sleep."

He said this more harshly than he'd intended, but he couldn't help it. She'd scared the shit out of him. His heart beat hard enough to bruise his ribcage. Adrenaline screamed through his veins, causing him to shake. He closed his eyes, doubting he would be able to sleep, but trying anyway, and then opened them again moments later to see the girl in the same position as before, that smile still curving her mouth. Neon danced with the shadows on her face, making it look less than human.

Shit. What's her name again? Damon thought. *Katrina? No. It was something unusual.* He searched his memory, wading through the booze, fear and fog. *Kira? Yeah, that's it.* They'd only met a few hours before at a local punk show. She was twenty-one, six years his junior, and one of the best lays he'd ever had. Not because she was skilled or kinky, but the opposite—they were both piss ass drunk and the sex had been a sloppy, fumbling, beautiful mess.

"I just came back from the most amazing show," she said again in that dazed, dream whisper.

"Yes we *did*," Damon said slowly, as if speaking to a child.

The headlining band was called The Blind Dead after some low-budget Spanish horror film. The bar had been packed to capacity, shoulders brushing shoulders, the atmosphere heavy with the musk of cheap weed and body odor.

Once the band started, the bar's shitty sound system could barely handle the volume. The guitar sounded like a bag of cats thrown into a wood chipper, yet the crowd managed to dance anyway. Well, maybe dance wasn't the right word. They *moved* their bodies in synch with the music, limbs loose and boneless, heads banging. The inevitable mosh pit erupted at the foot of the stage and rapidly metastasized throughout the crowd.

Before he knew it Damon had been absorbed by the collective, becoming a single cell in a much bigger organism. He rubbed against friends and strangers, their heat absorbed into the fabric of his clothing, his skin. Closing his eyes, the world spun and twisted like he was the center of a galaxy gone haywire.

When his eyelids peeled open, he saw Kira, her head lolling to the music, face shining with sweat that reflected the bar's scanty light. She smelled unwashed, earthy and primal. His senses nearly short-circuited. His nostrils brimmed with her scent. His eardrums throbbed with the band's gunfire drumming. And soon his mouth was filled with the taste of Kira's tongue as she stumbled toward him and placed an unexpected kiss on his lips. All in all it was a pretty good—

"Not that show," Kira said, bringing Damon back to the neon-tinted darkness.

He shook the memories of that evening from his mind and realized he was having trouble reconciling the Kira from the bar with the one looking down at him now, grinning feverishly and bathed in crimson light. It was like he'd gone to bed with one woman and woken up with another. *Only this one isn't exactly a woman, is she now, Damon? Shut the fuck up*, he told the nagging Vincent Price voice in his head.

Damon hated anything even remotely scary. He still watched horror films through the spaces between his fingers. Whenever he was alone that voice—the one that sounded oddly like Vincent Price—would bubble up from his subconscious and fill him with suggestions of what might be lurking in the corners where the shadows were darkest. *Perhaps a blood-crazed murderer found his way into your apartment while you were at work*, or, *this building is old, who knows how many spirits call it their home*. The voice was having a field day now, composing an entire *Thriller*-style rhapsody about Kira's odd behavior. Damon did his best to ignore it.

The voice of rationality strove to overpower the fear. *Obviously Kira is a sleep walker*, it said, informed by a wrinkled lifestyle magazine Damon had flipped through once while waiting at the doctor's office.

Otherwise known as somnambulism, he now remembered—a word he associated with coffins and shambling white-faced weir-does—*the people afflicted appeared to be sleeping with their eyes open, while their minds were still submerged in the mire of dreams*. They were basically puppets to their own subconscious. The thought didn't reassure him. It had the opposite effect, sending a fresh chill down his back. He decided to steer his mind in a different direction. At this rate, he was careening toward full-bodied panic.

"What show?" he asked, thinking it was better to focus on the little details than the bigger picture, with its horror movie implications.

Kira's jaw unlocked and her lips began forming words normally. It was like watching her come awake from paralyzing sleep. Only Damon wasn't convinced she was actually awake. That dream puppeteer was still tilting his control bar in some far-off place, guiding her strings with a deft hand.

"They didn't have a name," she said. "I don't remember them playing any instruments either, but I heard them."

Damon frowned. To humor her, he asked, "What venue?"

"It was a basement show. I've never been there before."

For some reason, this vague response triggered a mental image so vivid Damon thought he'd been transported to the basement in question. It was low ceilinged, musty with dust and the smell of damp. The walls were patterned with oblong patches of paint a shade darker than the rest, as though band posters had once adorned them but had long since been removed. When the image blinked out of existence, Damon experienced a brief spell of vertigo.

When he recovered, he said, "What kind of music was it?"

"Punk. Their sound was raw and violent. I could feel it in my blood like contact dye."

And that's enough for me, Damon thought. He was too tired and overwrought to listen to this bullshit any longer. To make matters worse, a headache rapped on his skull, demanding entry. He wanted to sleep and for that to happen, he needed Kira to snap out of it.

Impatience crept into his voice. "What the hell are you talking about? Go to sleep. You're freaking me out."

Kira didn't go back to sleep. She stood up, swaying on the lumpy mattress, and started dancing to a beat she heard only in her head. Her feet were bare, filthy, the polish chipped. Damon couldn't remember if she'd been wearing shoes on their walk home, or if she'd taken them off before entering the apartment. He was about to ask her when another scenario entered his mind. What if she'd actually snuck out in the middle of the night, shitfaced and disoriented, to an after hours basement show? Damon had drunk enough beer and done enough drugs to tranquilize him into a skid-coma, so it wasn't impossible that she slipped away without his notice.

Bleary-eyed, he peered across the room at the alarm clock. It was four twenty-seven. When did they get home? Two-thirty?

Did that give her enough time to hit another show and make it back in time to scare the shit out of him? He guessed so, assuming the clock was right. It had a habit of slowing down or speeding up on its own, so he couldn't be sure. Then again, how did she manage to get back into the apartment without a key? Did she pocket his only set before leaving?

Instead of asking her outright, he said, "Kira, are you fucking with me?"

She said nothing for several seconds. Then her impossible smile returned, stretching her face beyond recognition. Damon's bowels turned to water.

2. An Orgy of Infrasound

A finger jabbed him in the ribs. Damon jumped, startled, and looked up to see his best friend, Cid, pounding back a beer. He was no longer in his apartment. That much was obvious. The light was different, so was the musty, dirty sock smell.

They were sitting across from each other at a small, circular table. The window at Cid's back framed a night scene of street lamps and wet glistening asphalt. A pinball machine chimed and flashed in the corner. They were inside a bar, the same bar where Damon had seen The Blind Dead with Kira. Was that yesterday, or the night before? He couldn't remember. It felt like only seconds ago he'd been watching Kira's face twist into that unnatural grin. *Am I losing my fucking mind,* he thought with a stab of anxiety.

"*Hey, man. You all plugged in up there?*" Cid said tilting his head to one side like a confused lapdog. It sounded like he was speaking underwater.

Damon blinked a few times, trying to hit the reboot button on his brain. When Cid spoke again, his words sounded clear and Damon was relieved.

"You alright bud?" Cid asked.

"Yeah, yeah, I'm fine. I just sort of zoned out, I guess."

"What's the last thing you remember me saying?"

Damon's silence was answer enough. He didn't remember a fucking thing. It was awkward and more than a little troubling, but there was no point hiding the fact. He shrugged his shoulders and scrunched up his face by way of apology.

Cid laughed. "Jesus. Are you high?"

"No." Damon shook his head. "I don't know. Just confused and tired. I didn't get much sleep last night." But he wasn't convinced that was the truth. He wasn't convinced of anything.

A distorted guitar riff tore through his head, blotting out the world. He saw Kira, her too-wide smile and the silhouette of concert performers he somehow identified as the nameless band she'd mentioned. The sudden onslaught of images made him flinch. Were these fragments of a memory or a dream? If he thought too hard about it, a sharp pain started at the base of his skull. Maybe he *was* high, had been dosed with something—roofies, acid, or a new grifted pharmaceutical that worked its way into the scene. What else could explain his disorientation?

"All good, man," Cid said and grinned sideways. He gestured to the full glass of beer in front of Damon. "Have a drink. Relax. You didn't miss much. I was ranting about my usual paranoid bullshit."

Damon lifted the glass to his lips, a patient taking his medicine. The taste was familiar and comforting. The world started to make sense again.

He looked at Cid like he was seeing him for the first time. He was dressed in his usual uniform: faded boot cut Levi's, nondescript black t-shirt, and black jean jacket adorned with pins and patches. Most of these were logos of his favorite punk and metal bands, others allusions to obscure cult horror films. His hair was self-cut and unkempt and he smelled like cigarettes and an undercurrent of—what was it? Rotten meat? No, that couldn't be right. Damon sucked in another breath through his nose. The smell, whatever it had been, was gone. All that remained was the spectral trace of stale cigarette smoke.

"Ever hear of MKUltra?" Cid asked.

Damon shook his head. Over Cid's shoulder, he could see the street, deserted and dark. The sky didn't look right, but Damon couldn't put his finger on why. Before he could get to the root of his observation, Cid's voice reeled him back in.

"It was the code name for a bunch of secret research projects led by the government in the fifties and sixties. Mind control shit. Most of the test subjects didn't even know they were part of an experiment. They were involuntarily dosed with LSD, hypnotized and tortured—all kinds of fucked up shit." Cid was getting more and more agitated with every word. Now that he was finished, though, his demeanor had relaxed and he stared absently around the room. Then, finally, he faced Damon again and said, in the calmest tone imaginable, "It's all declassified now. You can read some of the original documents online."

Damon fought hard to suppress the bubbles of anxiety rising up within him. It was like Cid had been reading his thoughts, tuning into his paranoia. *What if I told you, Damon, that you were a test subject in an underground experiment,* said the Vincent Price voice. *Why else would you remember this conversation? Yes, I said remember. You aren't experiencing this interaction in real time. You're remembering it.* Price let out his trademark cackle, rising waves of sinister laughter pounding through Damon's skull. He shoved the imaginary voice aside like he would a drunken asshole bumping into him at the bar.

"Sure," he said to Cid. "What are you getting at?"

Cid spread his hands as if to say, "Hold on a sec, I'm trying to get to the point here." He took another pull of his beer, careful to replace the bottle in the ring of condensation it formed on the table when he was finished, and resumed what was shaping up to be one of his many, wild conspiracy theories. Damon knew what he was going to say before the words came out of his mouth.

"I don't think these mind control experiments ever stopped," Cid said, leaning forward, his chest pressed against the table's edge.

"What do you mean?"

"I've been picking up on these signals. The air around us is a total orgy of infrasound."

A frown creased Damon's forehead.

Cid stuttered out an explanation, "Infrasound is an extremely low frequency sound, way below the limit of human hearing. It's everywhere. You're picking up on it now without even being aware of it, but I managed to train myself to tune in and hear specific voices stealthily designed to target the subconscious mind."

This statement did little to ease Damon's anxiety, conspiracy bullshit or no. He wasn't right in the head, and anything Cid could have told him would have driven another nail of paranoia into his already quivering brain. And the Vincent Price voice only got louder as the conversation continued: *Is this reality? Or is it a dream? In this sleep of death, what dreams may come? Ha-ha-ha-ha-ha-ha!*

Goddamnit, shut the fuck up, Damon thought desperately.

Another guitar riff drowned out his senses, followed by a second flash of the nameless band in silhouette. A lead singer, bassist, guitarist and drummer, all of them physically distorted like they were originally one vast shape struggling to remain separated. They kept phasing into one another, their outlines trembling and blurring. Damon blinked hard.

When the hallucinations subsided, he tuned briefly back into reality, catching only snippets of Cid's monologue, "…project 68…using cues to trigger…almost hypnotic alpha wave state…controlled doses of alcohol and marijuana."

He shook his head to clear it. Nausea bloomed in his stomach like a poisonous flower. He had a sudden, vivid image of himself puking blood on the table. The thick, red fluid filled his glass. It overflowed, pouring from the edges of the table in noisy streams, spattering the floor and his shoes. Cid's face was flecked with gore, but he still rambled, on and on and on and on.

Another riff, and this time Damon thought he could hear other instruments under the steady thrumming, whine of the guitar. Punk music. The sound was raw and primal. It was the only way he knew how to describe it, using the same words Kira had whispered to him that night. When was that? Yesterday? Last month? Last year? Had it even happened?

The music rose in pitch. Crunchy guitar chords ripped through his head, cymbals crashed against his eardrums, and a voice that couldn't possibly be human wailed into a voice amplifier: *You're all fucking filth,* it sang, *You all deserve to die / Cut yourselves open / Take everything out / Put it on the table.*

A loud pop and Damon was back. Cid rambled on as if nothing had happened, "They're targeting counterculture movements, minorities," he was saying. "Queers, immigrants, hippies with an allergy to bathing, you name it."

The lyrics still echoed in Damon's mind as he said, "Counterculture movements? What are you talking about? Who's targeting them?"

"You drifting off again, man? It's the government. All those old pissed off white dudes who can't roll with the times. They've developed sonic weapons and they've found a way to sneak them into our music. The punk scene is an easy target with its fury and anarchic sentiment. I think they're going to wipe us out first."

"This sounds fucking insane. Even for you, Cid," Damon said. The lyrics had faded into silence, leaving him with a deep feeling of unease. "What do the weapons do? How do they get them into our music?"

"I'm not exactly sure, but maybe the musicians are already infected and unwittingly emit some kind of infrasound frequency."

"Infected?"

"Yeah, the weapons cause tumors to develop in the ear canals, tumors that'll gain sentience and worm their way into the brain, ultimately controlling the host like a puppet. Soon they'll blast signals"—Cid jabbed a finger in the air like he was firing a laser beam from under his fingernail—"into the decision-making part of the brain, compelling the host to surgically remove parts of their body until they're an empty sack of skin controlled by the earworms."

The lyrics repeated in Damon's memory: *You're all fucking filth / You all deserve to die / Cut yourselves open / Take everything out / Put it on the table.* What was going on? Was this some kind of sick joke? Everything Cid described matched perfectly with what was happening to him. *Holy fuck,* he thought, *I am losing my mind.*

"The act of removing one's body parts, in this case, is called a Transhuman Panotomy. Get it? Transcending humanity by removing everything that makes you human. That's the delusion. You're going to remove everything and die. You're not going to transcend to some loftier state of existence like the earworms are promising you, *you're going to fucking die.*"

"Is the nameless band one of these sonic weapons?" The words dribbled out of Damon's mouth like an involuntary gush of vomit.

"You know about that?" Cid said, his shock palpable.

I just came back from the most amazing show.

"What can you tell me about them?"

"Not much," Cid admitted. "They're part of all this, though.

Ground zero. Something horrible in the shape of a band that speaks in punk music tones. They're dangerous, man. I don't think any of us can really understand what they're all about."

Damon was listening, but staring outside the window over Cid's shoulder. He finally realized what was wrong with the sky. It was fake, a matte background on a cheap movie set. He wasn't inside a bar. This wasn't reality, or a memory—it was hell.

"Why?" Cid said. "Do you know someone who's seen them?"

3. Transhuman Panotomy

"You fell asleep on me."

Damon reluctantly opened his eyes and saw Kira perched over him, her face a shadow one minute and a mask of red light the next. She still wore the same predatory smile. A whimper rose in Damon's throat, threatening to break free. He tried to swallow it down, but it lodged there like a stone. Kira cupped his cheek and stroked the hair on his temple with her fingertips, humming some tune, a very familiar tune.

"You were having a bad dream," Kira cooed.

Damon threw her off him and she hit the wall with a soft thump. He skidded up to his feet and ran, stumbling, toward the bathroom. Slamming and locking the door behind him, he turned and stared at his reflection in the mirror.

"Okay," he breathed. "You're awake." He punched his forehead hard enough for his vision to blur momentarily. "You're real. Flesh and blood."

Using his thumb and forefinger, he peeled back his eyelid and examined the pupil for any sign of drug reaction. It shrank in the light. But that didn't necessarily rule out the possibility of drugs. Maybe if he forced himself to vomit, it would clean out his system. Like that one time, during a bad mushroom trip, when he—

Movement from the edge of his vision. Looking down, he saw a black and segmented thing slither down the drain. Its body was mottled with blind milky eyes—or were they mouths?—that seemed to possess a dull sort of intelligence.

Woozy dread trickled along Damon's nerves. Then he screamed until he tasted blood in his throat as a supernova ignited in his skull. The agony was brief but apocalyptic, the worst headache imaginable. When he looked in the mirror again, his left ear was gushing blood. A dark red stream painted a swath down his jawline, neck and shoulders.

Outside the door, muffled but unmistakable, came the whispered tones of Kira's voice. "They're making babies inside your brain," she said. "Little souvenirs from the nameless band." She giggled. Her feet beat against the floor in rhythmic cadence. She was dancing.

Damon gripped the sides of his head with shaking hands, not wanting to believe what she had told him. Somewhere music started to play. Savage drumbeats gave way to dirty guitar chords and lyrics: *You're all fucking filth / You deserve to die / Cut yourselves open / Take everything out / Put it on the table.*

It was coming from inside the walls. Damon clamped his hands over his ears, one palm sliding against the steady rush of blood. Under the music, he heard a gnawing sound from inside his own skull, like cereal crackling in freshly poured milk, and knew it was the tumors, the earworms, feasting on his brain tissue.

A knock on the door. "Let me in, Damon. Let's dance."

"Fuck off," he screamed.

"Fine. I'll start without you." A pause that seemed to last forever. "You keep the knives in the first drawer, right?"

Damon slammed the door with an open palm, leaving a bloody handprint. "Don't even think about it, don't you fucking dare."

The music heightened in volume until Damon's teeth vibrated and a wave of dizziness washed over him. He had no other choice. He couldn't allow Kira to slice her body open. He clutched the door handle, hesitated.

"Fuck me."

He twisted the knob and the door opened, but the apartment outside was no longer familiar. The floors were raw cement, the walls painted an unsightly brown, like liquid shit. A single tube of fluorescent light—the others were dead husks—illuminated the space. The air smelled like a slaughterhouse.

"Kira," he screamed, but his voice was drowned out by the music, louder now that the door was open. It was coming from somewhere down the hallway.

He took a step onto the cement floor, cold under his bare feet, and shivered. For the first time tonight he realized he was completely naked. A bolt of panic surged through him. Cupping his dick and balls with bloody hands, he cautiously made his way down the hallway, toward the music. At what seemed like halfway, he noticed he was singing along with the band, pausing between every line to utter a hoarse explosion of laughter.

At the end of the hallway, he rounded a corner and found himself in a familiar room. The atmosphere was musty and the ghosts of band posters haunted the walls. It was the basement where Kira had seen the nameless band.

Kira was standing next to an old wooden table, the room's only piece of furniture, a blood-caked knife gripped in one hand. A jagged incision ran from below her breasts down to where her pubic hair started. Her intestines spooled out on the floor, steaming in the cold air.

She smiled at him, her mouth awash in red, and raised the knife in greeting. A black worm squeezed out of her ear and slapped wetly on the floor.

"Let's transcend together," she said, but it didn't sound like Kira. The voice was oddly musical and crackly like an old record.

Kira took a step toward him, her bare foot nudging a coil of intestines across the gritty cement. She reached into the incision and pulled out something that may have been her liver, lifted it to her nose, inhaled its muggy, fleshy aroma, and took a bite. It looked tough, resisting the pressure of her jaws. Blood and clear fluid squirted out on her face and forearm. After some effort, she managed to tear off a piece and started to chew, her eyes rolled to whites.

Damon didn't even scream. The shock was so deep he could only turn and walk briskly in the direction he'd come. His head was down and not three steps away he bumped into another person. He looked up and stared into the ravaged face of his best friend. Cid smiled, exposing a mouth void of teeth and tongue. Even some of the gums had been scraped away like the guts from inside a pumpkin. Damon spared a glance down. Cid's stomach was slashed wide open, the edges of the incision curling outwards. The cavity was empty and the ridges of his spinal column were visible at the back.

Damon's eyes returned to Cid's face and started to film with tears as worms wriggled in profusion from Cid's eye sockets, pushing the orbs outward until they popped free and dangled against his cheeks from their optic nerves. In their place, the worms balled up and formed ersatz eyes that gleamed blackly in the dim light.

Cid proffered his knife and Damon accepted it in a trembling hand. He was still singing along to the music. Cid's lips were moving too, but no sound emerged. To a combined chorus of the nameless band and the worms gnawing away at his brain, Damon pressed the knife into the soft tissue of his abdomen.

CYBERPUNK ZOMBIE JIHAD

BY MARK ZIRBEL

The following article appeared in Industrial Underground magazine, Vol. 5, No. 7.

BAND SPOTLIGHT: crashdump
Front man Madd0x N1x0n is part man, part machine, part zombie —and ALL punk!

Interview by Jason Connelly

It's strange to consider that if Madd0x N1x0n had lived in a different era, his death by heroin overdose would have been the end—the end of his life, the end of his music, the end of his legacy. Fortunately for us, N1x0n hit the music scene during the Great Holy War, so his death two years ago was only the beginning of his story.

The events following N1x0n's death were SOP: his corpse was seized by the government, reanimated, and sent to a military black site for combat conditioning. But N1x0n, who had bucked the system for years with his cyberpunk band crashdump, had a surprise up his sleeve:

He was a Selfer.

For those of you living under a rock, Selfers are the 1% anomalies in the population who retain their human consciousness after reanimation. N1x0n wisely didn't let on about his condition, shambling his way through countless suicide commando drills along with thousands of other conscripted corpses. Finally, an opportunity presented itself for N1x0n to give his trainers the slip before they could ship him off to the Middle East.

These days, N1x0n is back with crashdump (N1x0n – vocals, sound manipulation; Alexx I/O – synths, programming; Pig – guitar, bass; Jackson Blades – drums), creating politically charged noise rock again. Although a daily concoction of black market preservation drugs minimizes his decomposition, a certain amount of decay is inevitable for N1x0n. As parts of his body have rotted away, he's replaced them with a variety of robotics and machinery. Being the creative genius that he is, he's even found a way to incorporate these mechanisms into his music—making it more pulverizing than ever!

Industrial Underground is proud to present an exclusive interview with Madd0x N1x0n.

IU: So, do you think you can make it through this interview without eating me?

MN: *(grinning)* I'll do my best. That's one thing all those fucking movies got wrong, isn't it? They always showed the lamebrains chowing down on flesh and guts. Turns out they don't eat a goddamn thing!

IU: That's true of all zombies? Even a Selfer like you?

MN: *(laughs)* Sorry … I always crack up when I hear that word. When I was a teenager, that's what we called those guys in pornos who suck their own schlongs! I'm definitely *not* a Selfer in that sense! But, to answer your question, I don't eat anything. What's the fucking point in shoveling food down my throat when I don't have a functioning digestive system? Plus, my taste buds are dead, so there's no enjoyment in it anyway.

IU: That sucks. How's your health overall?

MN: I feel like I'm more machine than man these days. But I'm hanging in there.

IU: How many mechanical parts do you have at this point?

MN: Let's see … right eye, jaw, right hand, left arm, abdomen, and left leg. I've still got my penis, though. Thank god for that—and for Viagra!

IU: Viagra? Really?

MN: Yeah. Ever since my reanimation, I've needed a little help with the ladies. But, hey, I'm still doing pretty goddamned good for a dead guy!

IU: I'm amazed that you have a sense of humor about all of this. How do you maintain such a positive attitude after everything you've been through?

MN: I'm living on borrowed time, so why not raise some hell? If I had come back as a lame-o like most people do, I would've lasted a couple of months at best. Those fascist pigs were planning to shoot me full of smallpox and set me loose in a Damascus marketplace!

IU: Wait a minute! I thought our military was using zombies as improvised explosive devices—sending them into combat zones strapped full of explosives. We're using them as biological weapons too? And we're targeting civilians?

MN: Yep. And smallpox is the least of what those sadists are cooking up. You wouldn't believe the things I saw at that government base. I gave a full debriefing to the leaders of the Resistance, so I'm not gonna rehash it all here. But I'll tell you this: That hellhole is the last place on earth where you ever want to find yourself!

Jason wakes up in suffocating darkness—*literally* suffocating, thick fabric clinging to his sweaty face. He tries to remove it but his hands are locked in place. Can't move … can't breathe … hyperventilating. Each of his staccato breaths comes back hot and stale, recirculating within the tight confines of his hood.

Despite his confusion, Jason recalls being jumped outside his apartment—two goons hooding him and shoving him into the back of a van. No memories after that. The throbbing pain in the back of his head tells him he was knocked unconscious.

How long was I out? Where am I now? Why the hell can't I move?
CALM … THE FUCK … DOWN.

Easier said than done, but Jason knows it's his only option—unless he wants to die from a panic attack. He forces himself to assess his situation as calmly as he can. He's sitting in a hard chair. He feels cold metal against his skin … feels it on his back, his buttocks, his thighs …

Oh, fuck …

Jason suddenly realizes the totality of his helplessness—he's naked and bound, metal clamps holding his arms and legs firmly in place. As a fresh wave of dread spreads over Jason, he hears a door open and close. Footsteps approach, continue just past him, and then stop. A voice comes from directly behind him: "This is a very nasty situation you're in, Mr. Connelly. Your cooperation will go a long way."

Without warning, the hood is yanked off Jason's head. His immediate instinct is to turn around, but as he begins to do so, a sharp "NO!" halts him.

"Eyes forward, Mr. Connelly. Everything you need to see is right in front of you."

There's a long, metal cart in front of Jason's chair. From his seated position, Jason is at eye level with the items on the top shelf: a hammer and nails, pliers, blowtorch, drill, and boxcutter.

A black-gloved hand shoves the latest issue of Industrial Underground under Jason's nose. The cover photo is a headshot of Maddox Nixon, flashing a menacing-looking grin courtesy of his rusted-metal jawpiece. The headline: A CONVERSATION WITH MADD0X N1X0N: AMERICA'S MOST WANTED, INDUSTRIAL'S MOST EXTREME.

"I want to find Maddox Nixon, Mr. Connelly. Where did you interview him?"

Staring at the face of his friend, Jason is determined – despite his fear – that he won't give him up. A lie pops into his head and he goes with it. "It was a Skype interview. That's how we conduct all our interviews at IU. I have no idea where Maddox is."

"That's interesting. So, at the beginning of the interview, when you joked about Maddox eating you, how was he going to do that, exactly? Attack you through your computer monitor?"

Shit. Jason should have removed that exchange from the interview. It was the only thing that gave away that he talked with Maddox face to face.

"Despite your efforts to conduct the interview as if you and Maddox were strangers, I know that the two of you go way back.

I know that you're trying to protect him. But there's no need! Here … let me show you something."

Jason's mystery interrogator steps in front of him for the first time. He wears a peaked military cap and a black overcoat with an American flag armband. Framing his minister's collar, a silver "M" gleams from one of his lapels, an "F" from the other—the symbols of the government's infamous Ministry of Fear. The man cuts such an imposing figure that it takes Jason a second to notice his face. Dear god … his face …

It's rotting.

For all the time he's spent around Maddox, Jason should be used to the sight of decomposing flesh. But there's something different about this man's state of decay. His skin looks yellowed and gloppy, falling from his face in wet chunks, exposing random patches of gory muscle and a skeletal jawline.

"I am Reverend-Commander Heinz, and I'm a Selfer—just like Maddox Nixon. I believe that Selfers are the key to achieving victory in the Great Holy War. An army of mindless drones is fine, but give me ten divisions of soldiers who are undead *and intelligent*, and I'll make the desert flow with rivers of blood." He makes the sign of the cross, adding, "Thy will be done."

Jason forces himself to look at Heinz's cottage cheese-like face, staring right into the grotesque eyeballs that bulge through the lumpy mess. "Look … I've already told you. I don't know where Maddox is."

"And I'm quite certain that you're lying. That's why I want to assure you that no harm will come to your friend. We simply want to study him so we can unlock the mystery of Selfers and learn how to make more of them. I've willingly submitted to a battery of tests myself—with minimal side effects, as you can see," Heinz says, running a hand before his face.

"Fuck you," Jason says. He nods toward the cart full of torture implements. "Give me your best shot, asshole."

Heinz chuckles. "Those won't be necessary. I have what I need to make you talk right here, Mr. Connelly." He reaches into his coat pocket and pulls out a CD case. He holds it so Jason can see the cover.

It's a copy of *Mile High Treason*.

The latest release from crashdump.

IU: Okay, let's talk music! Your new album, *Mile High Treason*, is available in hard copy formats only. What's the story behind that?

MN: With all the government spyware out there, too many of our fans are being monitored and harassed when they download our music. So we're blowing away the digital trail! Now, people can safely buy *Mile High Treason* on CD or vinyl at an underground record store or at one of our gigs.

IU: I'm amazed that you're still performing live! How is that possible for a band whose front man is on the FBI's Most Wanted list?

MN: We keep our gigs on the down low: unscheduled, unannounced, unadvertised. We jump around from town to town, playing in an abandoned warehouse one night, the basement of a liquor store the next. Word spreads fast among our hardcore fans. At our last gig, more than 300 people were crammed into this tiny crapshack out in the boonies. It was fucking insane!

IU: Aren't you worried that there could be a spy in the crowd?

MN: It's a pretty tight scene, so if somebody shows up who's never been around before, our security guys give them a close look. But, hey—if I get caught, I get caught. I can't sit around in the studio twiddling knobs forever. I gotta get out there in front of the fans!

IU: Since your shows are spur-of-the-moment events, it must be helpful that you carry a lot of your equipment on you wherever you go.

MN: When I found out four months ago that I was gonna lose my entire arm, the thought of replacing it with generic robotics seemed like a missed opportunity. So we custom-designed an arm-piece that has a sampler, a harsh-noise generator, a vocal processor, and a tape echo unit built right in.

IU: You're a one-man industrial sound machine!

MN: My other parts make some cool noise effects, too—like the motors and pistons and shit in my robotic leg. When they get going full bore, it sounds really ominous—like some kind of whirring death machine. So I sampled them and worked them into some of the songs on *Mile High Treason*.

IU: Tell us about the new album. What are some words you'd use to describe it?

MN: Loud. Corrosive. Discordant. Vicious. Chaotic.

IU: I'd add "Brilliant" to that list.

MN: Well, I don't know about that, but thanks.

IU: Is it safe to say this is your bleakest album to date?

MN: It's aggressive music for aggressive times. It's a call to war. It's a soundtrack for the apocalypse. It's motherfucking crashdump!

Reverend-Commander Heinz places the copy of *Mile High Treason* on the cart in front of Jason. It's a relief to get the blasphemous thing out of his hand, with its sickening cover art depicting his blessed Commander in Chief naked and bloody and impaled on a stake.

"So, you enjoy discordant music, do you?" Heinz asks Jason. "Let's see about that."

Heinz retrieves a small remote control device from his pants pocket and presses a button. A pair of 8-foot speakers slowly descend from the ceiling via a motorized cable system. As Jason watches them come down, the Reverend-Commander relishes the renewed fear in his captive's eyes.

"What's wrong, Mr. Connelly? You were so bold a moment ago—so prepared for me to do my worst. But now, you're not so sure what my worst is, are you?"

The speakers touch ground on each side of Jason's chair, sandwiching him between two monoliths. Each speaker is aimed at the other, with Jason positioned to take the audio crossfire.

"Here's the thing, Mr. Connelly: I'm not going to torture you. Maddox Nixon is. You think his music is brilliant? You might not feel that way after being pummeled with it at 125 decibels." Heinz retrieves the copy of *Mile High Treason* and examines its back cover. "Let's see ... which song shall I play? Ah, this looks like a good one: 'Kill Her Children with Death.' With a playing time of 4 minutes and 53 seconds, it should be *just* short enough for you to avoid permanent hearing damage. Or maybe not. Whatever the case, we'll see if you feel like talking afterwards. If not, I can hit you with some more near-deafening blasts. Or, perhaps I'll try a subtler approach—like locking you in an eight-by-eight cell with *Mile High Treason* playing on a continuous loop: 80 decibels, 24 hours a day, day after day after day. You won't go deaf but you'll probably go mad. Can you imagine? Unable to sleep ... unable to *think*. That would be a terrible way to—"

Heinz is cut off by the sound of an explosion, close enough to rattle the walls and reverberate through the floor. Warning lights on the ceiling flash as a computer-generated voice comes through the intercom: "INTRUDER ALERT. INTRUDER ALERT. UNAUTHORIZED PERSONNEL DETECTED IN SECTOR B7. ALL AVAILABLE GUARDS RESPOND IMMEDIATELY. ALL AVAILABLE GUARDS TO SECTOR B7."

"I bet it's the Resistance!" Jason says. "Maddox told them all about this place. You bastards are fucked!"

Heinz is tempted to retort by pressing the Play button on his remote control. Nothing would make him happier than to see blood trickling down Jason's neck from his ruptured eardrums. But his fun will have to wait—Heinz needs to find out what the hell is going on. He hurries out the door without saying another word to Jason, leaving him naked and alone in the interrogation room.

As the Reverend-Commander dashes through the interrogation wing, he examines the day's duty roster in his mind. Eight guards are stationed in the immediate vicinity of Sector B7, all capable of getting there in less than 30 seconds. Suddenly, Heinz hears the sound of M4 carbine fire—his men are on the scene and responding! This prompts him to quicken his pace even more—if members of the Resistance were stupid enough to enter this base, he wants to be there to see them get their just desserts.

Heinz exits the interrogation wing and enters a connecting corridor that leads straight to his destination—just a hundred yards to go! As he begins his final sprint, the M4s are abruptly squelched by the sound of counter fire.

What the ...? How many of those sinful traitors have breached our defenses? It sounds like there's a full squad in there!

When Heinz reaches the far end of the corridor, the shooting has stopped. He pauses outside the door that leads into Sector B7, which is an open arena used for zombie training exercises. As the Reverend-Commander unholsters his M17 semi-automatic, he presses the remains of his maggot-eaten ear to the door. All is quiet inside: no gunfire … no voices … nothing.

Heinz takes a deep breath as he hovers a finger above the door's security control panel. "O God, my Father, I appeal to Your Divine Justice to grant me victory in the coming battle. I ask this in the name of the Lord of the Armies, my Savior, the Lord Jesus Christ. Amen."

He punches in a seven-digit code and the door slides open.

"Aw fuck me to hell," the Reverend-Commander mutters.

It's an abattoir inside.

On the near end of the room, the arms and legs and torsos and heads of Heinz's men lie scattered across the floor in pools of blood. On the far end of the room, piles of broken concrete and a giant hole in the wall reveal the point of entry for the assault. And who came through that hole? A squad of Resistance fighters? An entire platoon? No … there's just one man standing there … one man responsible for all this carnage.

"Maddox! You goddamned son of a bitch!" Heinz shouts.

A mini rocket launcher is perched atop each of the rock star's shoulders. He grips a machine gun with an under-barrel shotgun attachment in his robotic right hand, and his left arm-piece has been transformed into an enormous Gatling-style machine gun. All of Maddox's weapons have the ragtag look of Resistance creations, custom-built to deliver maximum bloodshed.

"If you had turned yourself in, I would have let you live," Heinz says. "Okay, it wouldn't have been much of a life—confined to a cell, subjected to endless tests and surgeries. But now, that's not an option. My superiors will insist that we put you down for this. Scores of reinforcements will be here in under a minute. You're done, Maddox. What do you have to say for yourself?"

Maddox shouts a reply. The acoustics in room must be bad … Heinz must not have heard him right. Because what the rock star said makes no sense.

"Come again?" Heinz asks.

Maddox repeats himself, speaking slowly and clearly.

Heinz *did* hear him correctly. *Has Maddox lost his mind? Why is he reciting some ridiculous rhyme?*

And then Heinz remembers what Maddox said at the end of his magazine interview.

Aha!

Heinz nods his understanding to Maddox.

Maddox begins laughing as he raises his weapons and points them at Heinz.

The Reverend-Commander closes his eyes, listening to Maddox repeat his silly verse, knowing it will be drowned out at any second by the roar of gunfire.

IU: Tell us something that our readers would be surprised to learn about you.

MN: I don't consider crashdump to be an industrial band. I think of us as punks playing electronic music. That's why I've always described our music as *cyberpunk*. And just like any great punk band, we're all about getting people to think for themselves. To question everything. To fucking *resist!* Hell, I'll end the band tomorrow and start tossing Molotov cocktails into government buildings if that's what it takes to wake people up.

IU: Are you serious?

MN: Dead serious—no pun intended.

IU: Is violence really the answer?

MN: J.G. Ballard had a great quote about violence. He called it an "evolutionary standby system, a last-resort device for throwing a wild joker into the game." Maybe I'm that joker.

IU: Rebellious music is one thing, but outright revolt will get you killed.

MN: So what? I'm ready to fight! Like I said before, I'm living on borrowed time anyway.

IU: If it comes to that, if the shit truly hits the fan, what do you want your last words to be?

MN: *(thinks for a moment and then grins)* I'm a joker, I'm a smoker, I'm an undead croaker!

I AM THE FUTURE

BY JOE QUENELL

The bottle exploded against the Lexus, webbing cracks across the rear windshield. Eric and Kate both screamed, ducking to avoid the blowback of shards. The eruption of breaking glass echoed throughout the parking garage. A bitter smell filled the air, reminding both of college parties and subsequent hangovers. A stream of malt liquor trickled toward the car's back bumper.

"*Suburbanites!*" the Deadbeat slurred, then cackled. He walked with the grace of a wrecking ball, his scrawny frame staggering between parked cars. He collapsed against a cherry SUV and wiped sick from his chin onto his sleeveless band shirt. Green dreadlocks sprouted from his scalp, masking his face. He scratched at a sore on his tattooed matchstick arm.

Eric's face reddened. He straightened and grit his teeth. His rage had been brewing since their passive-aggressive anniversary dinner. It festered during their silent walk from the steakhouse to the garage. Kate had been bracing herself for his average wine-induced temper tantrum. *How can you be so goddamn unhappy all the time when you don't have to work? I give you the world and you can't even smile?*

She'd hoped to make it home before the warfare started. Now Eric had a new target for his contempt.

"What the fuck, asshole?" he shouted, storming toward the Deadbeat. He pointed to the damaged window. "Are you going to pay for that? *Can* you? What the *hell's* the matter with you?"

"What's the matter with *you*?" The Deadbeat mocked in a forced Brooklynite drawl. "What's the matter with me? What's the matter with *matter?*"

Kate knew that line; a quote from some movie that she couldn't quite place. She glanced about the parking garage. To her left, an elevator, 50 feet away, leading to a shopping center. To her right, an expanse of parked cars, then a ramp shepherding to more vehicle-packed floors. Not a single bystander in sight. Nobody to intervene if things turned violent. She gripped her car keys and reached for Eric's shoulder with her free hand.

"Come on, Hon. Let's go. I'm sure insurance will cover the window."

Eric nudged her away, stepping closer to the Deadbeat.

"I'm sick of shitheads like you acting like you're above the law! Sleeping and pissing wherever you want. Parasites sucking off those who actually contribute!"

The Deadbeat pushed himself off the SUV. He parted the dreads from his pale, pockmarked face. A heavy-duty safety pin pierced his septum, collecting stalactites of dried snot. He snorted. Hocked a viscous, off-colored wad of phlegm into the air. Eric jumped back as it splattered onto the cement floor beside his Rockport loafer.

The Deadbeat raised his middle finger.

"Sit on this, *mothafucka!*"

Another quote. Kate thought of the punks she knew back in college. They'd been intelligent and, despite their extreme appearance, respectful. This asshole was an obnoxious caricature. The one-dimensional antagonist of a basic-cable TV show. Every time he spoke, a part of Kate hoped Eric would punch him out.

Eric raised fists and stormed the bum, ready to put a free trial of boxing lessons to the test. He wound up within a foot of the Deadbeat and swung a right hook.

The Deadbeat moved faster than any drunk should. He ducked Eric's punch and charged, driving a balled fist into Eric's gut. The blow siphoned the air from his lungs. Eric bent forward, gasping. The Deadbeat grabbed him by the lapels of his jacket and lifted him off his feet.

"You think this is a costume?" the Deadbeat growled. "This is a way of life!"

He swung his forehead into Eric's face. The collision echoed like a gunshot. Eric went limp. The Deadbeat released him and he toppled to the ground, lights out.

Kate screamed and bolted toward Eric, freezing as the Deadbeat laid wild eyes on her. She squeezed her keys tight with one hand and searched her trench coat pockets with the other, praying for her phone. Fuck. She'd left it on the coffee table at home.

The Deadbeat let loose a feral cackle and charged. His lips curled back into a leer, baring moss green teeth. Irises burnt like hot coals feeding hellfire. Kate forgot all about her phone and spun around, bee-lining for the Lexus with a scream. She thumbed the auto-lock button hanging from her keychain and pulled the driver's side door open, crawling in. She grabbed at the door handle but the Deadbeat intercepted before she could slam it shut.

Kate yelped and tried to crawl further into the car. The Deadbeat grasped her left arm with one hand and twisted the other into her blonde hair. He yanked, almost jarring her from her seat. Kate shrieked, gripping the wheel for dear life.

"Life is pain," the Deadbeat recited. "Pain is everything." He leaned in, teeth bared. *"You…you will learn."*

Kate grasped her car key like a knife and swung it into the Deadbeat's face. It entered his right eye with a sickening pop. He howled, releasing her. The keys jingled as he stumbled backward, grasping at his face. Kate slammed the door shut and hit the lock button, sucking back tears and fighting for breath.

The Deadbeat ripped the keys from his eye with a pained grunt and lobbed them across the garage. They ricocheted off the far wall with a reverberating ring. He charged at Kate's door and banged his fists against the window; blood and milky fluid pulsed from swollen eyelids. He wiped the gore from his face, smeared it onto the glass, and drew an A in the murky fluid. He traced a circle around it and spat in its center.

"*Fuck this!*" he bellowed, storming from the car. "*Let's do some crimes!*"

Kate knew that one. Repo Man.

A low moan came from outside the car. Kate glanced into the rear view mirror. Eric struggled to sit. He shifted, facing the Lexus. His nose was swollen twice its normal size and bent to the left. Blood streamed down his chin and splotched his white dress shirt. He tried standing and collapsed on his ass. Incoherent, concussed.

Kate crawled to the backseat and beat her fists against the cracked windshield. She screamed Eric's name until it felt like her vocal chords would rip. He glanced in her direction and some sense of recognition crossed his eyes. He tried standing again, but instead resigned to crawling on hands and knees. Kate wiped tears from her eyes as he made the slow trek toward the Lexus.

"Oh *please,* Eric, hurry! Come on, Hon! Please make it!"

The Deadbeat rushed Eric from the side and swung a combat boot into his face. Steel toes broke his teeth with a sickening crunch. Kate screamed louder, cried harder, beating her fists raw against the window.

Eric curled onto his side and coughed blood and teeth. The Deadbeat circled him like a vulture eyeing a carcass.

"Go on, Sidney," voice changing from Brooklyn thug to whiny Brit. "Slay the beast."

Another kick. Eric curled further inward and whined. The Deadbeat rolled him onto his back, bent down, and grasped his auburn hair.

"*Noooo, come on,*" voice now cockney, deep and dopey. "*Ee's a good dog.*"

Eric grunted out a sound between moan and sob. The bum straddled him and kneaded both hands in his hair.

"*Boooooooring, Sidney.*" Voice back to whiny. He lifted Eric's head off the ground—

"*Boring!*"

and dashed it against the concrete with all his strength

"*Boring!*"

again

"*Boring!*"

And again.

Kate covered her face with her hands and wailed. Eric squalled like a dying animal. There was a loud, wet smash, like a watermelon hitting asphalt. He went quiet. The Deadbeat cackled again.

"Exterrrrrminate!"

Kate wept, cursing a god that couldn't exist for allowing this.

Eric, she thought. *Oh fuck, baby, I'm so sorry.*

Every argument they'd ever had was now meaningless. She'd take a million of Eric's asshole moments if it brought him back to life, away from that…that monster.

A ding echoed through the garage, followed by the mechanical slide of elevator doors.

A moment of silence, followed by a scream.

Kate uncovered her eyes. A middle-aged woman stood paralyzed by the open doors, mouth agape. Her face paled to match the white of her tracksuit. Shopping bags slipped from her hands, their contents spilling across the ground.

Eric's head resembled an old pumpkin, smashed to fragments. The Deadbeat straddled him and fished a handful of gray matter from the mess. He picked away bits of scalp and skull, shoved the brain into his mouth, and chewed. Dipping his fingers into the pooling blood, he licked it off each digit, like a sauce. He shut his eyes, moaning with pleasure.

Kate climbed back to the driver's seat and unlocked the door. She cracked it open and began to yell.

"Help me! Please, you have to help me! He killed my boyfriend! He's going to kill me! *Please!*"

The Deadbeat turned to the woman and smiled. Bits of brain fell from his mouth.

The woman glanced from Kate to the Deadbeat. She took two shaky steps backward, shaking her head at the scene before her. Picking up her pace, she ran back into the elevator.

The Deadbeat leapt from Eric's corpse, howled, and charged. His boots left bloody waffle prints across the concrete.

"I am the future!" he screamed, Brooklyn once more. He stuck his boot between the elevator doors as they shut. Another loud ding and the doors pushed open; the Deadbeat pounced.

The woman's shrieks escalated to a level of terror Kate thought impossible. If she lived through this, they'd haunt her forever. She clamped hands over ears and imagined she was somewhere, *anywhere,* but here.

The screams died and the garage grew silent, save for the elevator doors opening, shutting. The woman's leg lay limp across the door's threshold. A pink croc dangled off her still foot.

Kate waited for the Deadbeat to leave the elevator. A minute passed. He remained. A foolish idea crossed her mind; her only real option other than remaining a sitting duck.

She had to get her keys.

They'd hit the far wall, but she hadn't seen where they'd landed. She'd have to be quick, quiet. She slipped off her heels and dropped them onto the seat beside her. Opening her door as gently as possible, she stepped onto the cold, concrete floor.

The wall sat 20 yards or so from the Lexus. Kate tiptoed towards it, scared to so much as take a breath. Chewing noises emanated from the elevator as she passed. She didn't dare peek in, nor did she look at Eric's remains. Staying focused, she tried to ignore the thickness of death tainting the air.

Crimson speckled the wall between a parked Chevy and a Subaru. Kate scanned the surrounding area, hoping the keys would be in plain sight. No such luck. She crouched low and peeked under vehicles. The keys rested under the Chevy, too far to reach. Kate cursed under her breath. She lay flat on her stomach and crawled under the truck, inching forward with arms and elbows. She angled her head sideways to avoid concussing herself on the frame rails. She snatched the keys once in reach and started backing out. Her lungs burnt with expired air she was too scared to exhale. She stood, dusted filth from her coat, and turned back toward the Lexus.

Something smacked her in the face and bounced to the ground. She yelped, clutched her nose, and stared down at the object.

A pink croc.

"*Happy Easter, asshole!*" the Deadbeat yelled, clutching his crotch and shaking. Gore saturated his skin and clothes. He swung his head back and howled before charging.

Kate's heart sank. There wasn't enough time to reach the Lexus before the Deadbeat intercepted. She backed up, turned, and broke into a full sprint in the opposite direction, to the heart of the garage. The road ahead curved upward toward a second floor, then a third. If she kept going she'd reach street level. She'd be free.

The thud of combat boots against pavement reverberated behind her. He was closing in. Kate threw the last of her energy into one final, useless push. The Deadbeat grabbed hold of her hair and yanked hard enough to rip bits of scalp free. Kate's stocking feet flew out from under her. She careened toward the ground, head rapping against concrete. Stars and static filled her vision. The bum straddled her, dangling the bit of scalp above her face, and hurriedly shoved it into his mouth, slurping the strands of hair down like spaghetti. He leaned close to Kate's face, leering through his good eye.

"Do you ever think about dying?" he asked in a woman's voice, shrill yet vicious. "You know, violently?" He balled his hands together, raised them above his head like a hammer of god. "And wonder, like, what would be the most horrible way to die?"

Kate flinched, weeping, waiting for blows to rain down.

They never came.

She squinted back to the Deadbeat. His body tense, his limbs rigid. He strained to keep from swinging his fists down. The rabid stare in his eye flickered out, replaced by fear. His face grew pale. Feverish. He spoke in a clipped whisper, the voice of a scared child.

"I-I know a life of crime led me to this sorry fate. And y-yet, I blame society. S-society made me what I am."

Repo Man again. Kate wasn't sure whether to struggle or call him a white suburban punk.

She didn't get long to think about it.

The Deadbeat vomited a torrent of black, oily sepsis all over her. It sluiced from his throat like an opened floodgate, stinking of beer, brine, infection. Splashing her face, it went into her mouth and down her throat while she screamed and thrashed. It soaked her clothing and burnt her skin.

And it ended as abrupt as it started. The stream shut off and the Deadbeat's weight subsided. He fell off of Kate, landed sideways on the ground. Kate sputtered and gagged, spitting out a mouthful of excretion. She wiped her eyes clean and peered at him.

Her jaw dropped.

His dreadlocks unraveled, losing their grimy matte. Their neon-green color faded, darkening to a natural brown. The amateur tattoos on his twig arms dissolved, as did the pock-marks scarring his face. The safety pin puncturing his septum shrank, bent, and broke. The metal fragments curled into his nose, disappearing from sight. The filth plastering his skin melted off into a brown puddle. He looked as clean cut as Eric. He closed his eyes, and a thin smile spread across his lips. He lay still. Kate placed a trembling hand on his cheek. It was cold.

She stood, wiped more vomit from her face, and started limping back toward the Lexus. Her lower back screamed with each step. Thinking about Eric, she choked back a sob, careful to avoid his remains as she passed.

The elevator door still opened and shut on the woman's plump body. One glance and Kate felt sick. Her nose, cheeks and right eye were missing from her face. Gore doused her white tracksuit, the pants pulled to her ankles. Weeping bites decorated doughy thighs. The Deadbeat had opened up her midsection like a Christmas present. Viscera trailed from her gut in an array of nauseating colors and textures. Kate gagged, turned away, and continued to the car.

She plopped down in the driver's seat and stuck the keys in the ignition, lowering her head and weeping before firing the engine to life. A familiar ring reminded her to fasten her seatbelt. She wiped tears from her face, put the car in reverse, and pulled out.

Music kicked in at an ear-splitting level. She slammed on her brakes with a yelp, tried lowering her stereo's volume. It wouldn't budge. A loud, simplistic drumbeat pummeled at a medium speed, out of place on XM's soft R&B station. A belligerent voice joined after a few measures, spewing a repetitious message:

"Sex. And. Violence. Sex. And. Violence."

The beat slammed into Kate's brain like a sledgehammer against drywall. She covered her ears. It failed to mute the racket. A piercing guitar sliced through the song's repeating verse. Something riled in Kate's stomach, ascending her throat. She spewed lukewarm foam into her lap. Malt liquor. Wiping sick off her face, Kate winced as something sharp jabbed her hand. She peered into the rear-view mirror and screamed.

Two steel points punctured the skin under her lip, leaking scarlet rivulets down her chin. The metal grew, looping and contorting into safety pins embedding each side of her mouth. Her straight teeth shifted into awkward angles. Enamel chipped and took on the brownish rot of a lifelong smoker. Her blonde bangs twisted together and matted into filthy locks. An algae stain leaked from her roots to the frayed tips, overtaking her natural color like dye in water.

The music sped up with her heartbeat. The singer's rasp became a shout.

"Sex and violence! Sex and violence! Sex and violence! Sex! And! Violence!"

The puncture marks on Kate's hand grew hot. The sensation spread to her wrist and forearm. She looked to her hand and screamed again. Black lines trailed down her arm, branching off into crude shapes. An A surrounded by a circle on the back of her hand. An inverted cross and pentagram below her elbow. A crooked tombstone on her shoulder, marked with the messages *Life Fast, Die* and *Scumfuck.*

A chorus of voices joined the song's redundant proclamation. Kate found herself chanting along. She wiped at grit layering her flesh. It adhered to her like second skin. She laughed, couldn't help it. Eyeing the mirror again, she cackled harder. The black lines spread to her cheeks, forming little arrows and teardrops under her eyes. She stuck out her tongue, blew a raspberry at her reflection.

Hunger replaced the nausea in her gut. She peered though the back window at Eric's remains. Her memories of him subsided. All she saw was meat. She stepped out of the car and waltzed across the garage to his body, where she scooped up a handful of brain and ate. Moaning in pleasure, she went for seconds.

She crawled back into the car after eating her fill. She'd be hungry again soon. She'd have to hunt. But first she needed beer to wash down the taste of yuppie. She'd loot a corner store for malt liquor, then start the prowl. There were a million ritzy restaurants in this city, all filled with suburbanites. She'd dine like royalty tonight.

The thing that used to be Kate nodded along to the blaring music and threw the car back into reverse. She backed over Eric's remains and sniggered at the sound of bones breaking under wheels. She swerved through the parking lot, up the inclines and toward the exit. Laying her foot on the gas pedal, feeling more alive than ever before.

"I am the future!" she screamed as she ripped out the garage and into the awaiting night.

ROLLED UP

BY EMMA ALICE JOHNSON

I'm rolled up inside a dirty shag rug in the graffiti-covered alley behind the club. A band is loading in, and they have to step on me to get from their van to the back door. Their footsteps carry the extra weight of their gear. It feels so good.

They don't know I'm here. That would ruin it. When people know I'm underfoot, their steps become too intentional. They avoid me, tiptoe lightly over me or stomp extra hard. It doesn't feel natural. It's better when they don't know.

A few people know I'm here of course. Rolling myself up in a rug and dragging myself to the backstage entrance of a seedy East Village punk club is not an option, so I have an arrangement with a couple guys to get me here and then unroll me at the end of the night. Plus there are a few regulars who got curious about the rolled up rug that appears in different places around the club a few times a week, so stained from footprints and grime that the orange and brown pattern is barely discernable. Not to mention the one woman whose high heel hit that sweet spot on my neck, right under my jaw, eliciting a groan of pleasure I couldn't contain. She unrolled me and kicked the shit out of me with those heels, calling me a pervert.

I'm not a pervert though. This isn't a fetish for me. It's not that simple. I don't get off on it sexually. How could I? Jacking off isn't an option when I'm rolled up so tight my arms are pinned to my sides. I get off on it emotionally. Sometimes it's so intense I cry, not because of the pain, but because of how it makes me feel. It's not like an out of body thing, not exactly, because I'm very much present in my self. However, my senses reach beyond the boundaries of my flesh. I may not be able to see, but I can feel and hear and smell everything that is happening around me, even if it's muffled. I'm omniscient in my rug.

Oh, there is the physical sensation too. It isn't painful, although I'm often left bruised and I have a permanent limp from an untreated ankle fracture. It's not like getting kicked. The rug dulls the impact, so it's just the weight, the pressure. I love the feel of feet hitting different parts of me. The weight of a body on my buttocks or where the back of my skull meets my spine sends heat through my veins.

That heat dissipates quickly after the band members grunt through the last of their load-in. I'm left only with the external heat. It's a warm night, and the rug amplifies the warmth. I'm sweating. My naked flesh is chafing against the rug backing. When I unroll, my skin will be red and imprinted with the blocky pattern. But I can't think about unrolling now. The evening has just begun.

The backstage door is closed with a click and suddenly there is silence. New York City silence, at least. This is the city that never sleeps, after all. It's alive at all hours. Or is it? The whir of traffic, shoes scuttling over sidewalks, conversations, music in the distance. The same people going the same places and doing the same things. I hear it every night, and it sounds so mechanical, so routine. Is this city as wild and alive as it promises, or are the routines just a little more exciting?

When the band starts to play, the back door cannot contain the music. It's that newer, faster version of punk. I've been coming here for eight years, more or less. Time isn't something I pay attention to. But I've been coming since the late '70s, and I'm amazed at how much this music has evolved in such a short time. I can't say I love it. I grew up in Tennessee, listening to country, before I hitchhiked here in the '60s. But I love the people. They are artsy and curious.

This new strain of punk though, this hardcore, it's especially exciting. Once in awhile I'll actually come to the club to see a band, if I can scrounge up the bills. When these hardcore bands play, the crowds do a thing they call slam dancing. They stomp and spin and smash into each other. I can't help but wish I could lay my rug right there in front of the stage and be part of it in my own way. Maybe someday.

The set is over fast and the band comes out once again to step on me. They are practically bouncing they are so energized. Their sweaty shirtless chests slap against each other as they give hard hugs. "Did you see how crazy that crowd was? They were jumping off the stage! I could have played all night!" Their BO is so strong it wafts down to me and I draw it in through my nostrils. They keep stepping on me because they cannot stand still. They don't know what to do with themselves.

The gruff voice of the club owner echoes out. "Clear the stage, assholes!"

They laugh and get to work, and once again I absorb those extra weighted steps. The heat in me is so intense it reaches out of my skin, penetrating the rug. Purple flames light up the darkness behind my eyelids.

My euphoria is cancelled out by a scent that swirls past my nose. Something smells off. It's not my BO, nor that of the band members. It's not the standard stink of the East Village, with its piles of garbage and unclean bodies packed together. Something truly smells off, like meat gone wet with rot.

The footsteps stop.

Wait, I hear one set of footsteps approaching. They come in an odd, stumbling cadence. Drunken footsteps, I think.

"Hey lady, are you okay?" one of the band members asks.

"What's wrong with her fucking face?" another whispers.

"It looks like it's falling off."

"Do you need an ambulance?"

There's a long pause and then an answer: "Amaraaaaaghhh!"

This last cry puts pins in my spine. There's so much pain in it, and anger, and... need? Hunger? I've never heard anything like it. The shuffling, off-kilter steps grow closer and the members of the band back up until they are all standing on me –one on my head, one on my upper back, one on my butt and one on my calves. I am their ground. I can feel them shaking. Their fear shakes down into me.

Another cry from the encroaching woman, and suddenly weight shifts above me. She has knocked one of the band members down and they are struggling on the rug. Their bodies move back and forth over me like a rolling pin.

"Get her off," her victim pleads.

The snapping of teeth is so loud, even louder than the thuds of a blunt object – a microphone stand maybe – against flesh. This has never happened before. I have never been beneath a bar fight. But is this a bar fight? Shouting, heavy breathing, blows to bodies, yes – but that gnashing of teeth? Who fights like that?

Now the teeth are not just clicking against each other. They have found something to latch onto. Human meat. I know that blood is soaking into my rug. This woman, is she a cannibal? Has she killed a member of the band? I listen for the others. I listen hard over the sound of chewing, but hear nothing. Did they flee into the club like cowards while their friend was eaten alive?

The pressure on my rug eases and I try to get control of my thoughts, because they don't make sense. Perhaps I dozed off and had a strange little nightmare. In the hot, dark cocoon of my rug, sometimes awake and asleep blend together. Never like this, but there's always a first time.

I laugh loudly. Too loudly. Maybe I want to be heard right now. Maybe I need to be unrolled and brought back into reality. And my laugh does get a response: scraping at my rug, the frantic scratching of fingernails against shag. Another sickening cry from this woman and I am suddenly scared.

I take a deep breath and my eyes water at the scent I pull in. It is the scent of death. I know that scent well. I live in a squat, not far from the club. A tower of tagged and broken bricks filled with drunks and junkies who die regularly and are rarely discovered in a timely manner. I once found an overdose case with needle in arm who had decayed so badly I wasn't sure if it was a man or a woman. I wrapped my hands in plastic bags and pulled that body down four flights of steps and across three city blocks to a dumpster where it could be found without bringing police into my home. All the way I sucked in the odor.

The smell now is even stronger, too strong to be coming from the dead band member above me or from the woman who attacked him. It's getting closer, carried by feet, many feet that drag loose against blacktop. Bare toes catch on potholes and cracks. Ankles twist and snap. I hear bodies fall and the farcical movement that might have been called walking gives way to crawling. I do not have to see to know that these are dead people, and they are coming.

Within seconds they are on me, and as hard as I try to convince myself that I am wrong, I cannot deny my senses. The death stink grips my stomach hard and bile bubbles up my throat. I choke it down as the dead gather above.

So many feet on my rug. They must be packed body to body, pressing against each other as they push against the back door of the club. I hear groans and decaying flesh banging against metal, scraping against brick. With each scratch, fingernails flip free and the last bits of flesh on fingertips peel away.

My spine cracks. Something pops in my shoulder. I have never had so much weight on me at once. I have to fight to breathe, but I cannot deny how good this feels. I'm being pressed into nothingness, but I am still here. And what would happen if I weren't? I'm the glue that bonds these maggoty feet to the Earth. Without me, they would float up into the night sky and explode.

I swear I can feel a crack make its way through my right forearm bone and I envision blue flames in the fissure. Those flames run through me, up to my skull, where there is another rupture on my left temple. Turn me to dust! Let me blow through this alleyway to live under the foot of every New Yorker!

A squeal of metal tells me the backstage door is being forced open against the weight of the walking dead mob.

"There's at least a hundred of them," a voice says.

"Can we push through?" another asks.

"We don't have a choice. Take this."

"A yardstick?"

"Well, I'm using the bat. I'll go first."

Wood strikes decaying flesh and the weight shifts above me. With every blow, the odor of death gets more powerful. Skulls are opened to release the gasses that have accumulated around fetid brains. It's so strong it sticks to the inside of my mouth and I can practically chew on it like gum. It blends with the taste of blood. Where am I bleeding from? Inside? Or did my teeth merely rip my cheeks?

The wild swinging causes the crowd of corpses to part, putting more weight on my head and my legs. Quick steps volley off my midsection as a small group of living people make their way through. I consider crying for help, but it would be useless. If my cry was even able to penetrate my rug and the anxious clacking of corpse teeth, what could those few living do? Drag me away from here? Away from the ecstasy of all these feet above me? As much as I know that my body is crumbling – Ah, there goes my other hip – I cannot concede. Let it crumble in ecstasy. There is no life after this.

The scent of death becomes overwhelming. This is a scent without a home. The bodies are decaying and can no longer hold it, so it swirls desperately through the air to me so I can suck it into my lungs and give it a new place to live.

There's a sound like meat being slapped into the display case at the deli, and then like a bucket of not-quite-liquid hitting blacktop. Insides are pouring out, and now there's a wetness to the clacking of dead teeth, a new slurping. And that moaning, there's an all-too-familiar tone there. Could they be experiencing the level of joy that I'm experiencing right now? There's a whipping against my rug, and I imagine intestines at the center of a tug of war, yellowed nails piercing the tissue and setting free the brown muck inside. The dead are no longer standing on me. They are writhing around above me, against each other. Movement is constant.

Did any of the living survive? I think not. If they had, the dead would have given chase. I hear a cracking from my torso. A rib, most likely. There's a stabbing when I breathe. Perhaps several ribs are broken. That's fine. How high are the dead piled above me? Three bodies deep at least. Five? Twenty? Am I at the bottom of a skyscraper of squirming dead New Yorkers? The thought almost takes me out of my body, to the top of this skyscraper. I live in every dead body brick that makes it. I am the foundation, and without me it is nothing. Tower into space on me.

The dead are roaring above me, and the air is growing thin. They have blocked off all oxygen. I am so wet. This is not just my sweat. My bones have burst through my body. I am truly being crushed! Outside viscera has soaked through the rug and now coats me too. I can feel its warm redness, lubing my body under this impossible weight. Has any human ever felt a sensation like this before?

My pierced lungs suck in a big breath. I can breathe again. No! My load is getting lighter. My tower is collapsing. Knees scraped to bone slide against blacktop away from me, a new excitement in their groaning. Something is calling them away. They are leaving, all of them, after some new ecstasy, taking mine away.

A skittering above me indicates one lingering corpse fingering through the matted shag of my rug in hopes of finding a bit of liver or brain, but even that one is soon gone and there is nothing above me aside from that hollow weight of my rug, my sacred shell. I've never felt such loss. Everything so quickly turned to nothing.

Nothing. A naked, broken man wrapped up in a rug in an alley.

I know that my unrollers are gone. Eaten alive or fled. I'm not getting out of here. I don't want to get out of here. There is no life for me after this.

It's done. At least it's done here. In the distance though: Alarms. Sirens. Doors slamming. Gunshots. Screams. This is New York City, and I swear to Christ it has never sounded more alive.

BASS SICK

BY ASHER ELLIS

Les Claypool. Dee Dee Ramone. Flea. These were the faces that stared back at Johnny Bungalow as he lay on his bed among the album art and sheet music in his cold, cramped, tomb-like apartment room. The posters and black-and-white photographs of Johnny's favorite bassists that stuck to the concrete walls did more than inspire these days. They taunted. They mocked. They abused Johnny's trust that his axe of lower octaves would one day give flight to the world in which these legends eternally resided. But Johnny never once felt the urge to rip the faces of Krist Novoselic or Mike Watt from his wall. For he knew something as well as any of the bass-men that owned space in his shrine. He knew the bass.

He knew about foundations. That paint without a canvas falls to the floor. That melody without rhythm is like a woman without a pulse. Perhaps that's what first attracted Johnny to the instrument all those years ago. He would never deny how utterly cool a clean, dry bass note sounded all on its own. And he'd always admit the joy he derived from creating percussion on strings whenever his fingers slapped out a solid line. But deep down, deeper than any note he could create with his hands,

Johnny knew the real reason a more glorifying band position never grabbed his attention like the four-stringer.

It was because no one ever really listens to the bass behind the shred of a guitar solo. The bass is taken for granted, assumed to always be there in the background. But you take the bass away, and all of a sudden…people notice.

Johnny punched the "stop" button on his stereo and apologetically put an abrupt end to Rancid's "White Knuckle Ride." Although he usually would never cut short a Matt Freeman solo, Johnny's itch was stronger than ever and daydreaming just wasn't going to soothe it today. The members of Narwhal weren't going to have to lug their own equipment anymore. And if Eddie or Buzz weren't ready to do anything about it, then it was up to Johnny Bungalow. The foundation. The canvas. The bassist.

And now Johnny felt like a complete asshole. Not that Narwhal had played a horrible set. In fact, Johnny had performed a flawless groove from start to finish during their six-song setlist. And the rest of the band had been on their game, too. On other nights everything would've felt exactly as it should, but Johnny had made himself a promise earlier today and look where he was now. Sitting on a barstool choking back bottom shelf whiskey while the headliner wailed away. Same minimal paycheck. Same minimal appreciation.

In the end, the quality of places like Hoo Hah's wasn't the problem. Even if it was a dive bar so low key that it couldn't afford to carry two types of whiskey, Johnny had ultimately grown to dig Hoo Hah's atmosphere. It attracted genuine audiences, true rockers who could deal with having to take three subways to hear some great music. And Marty, the burnt out ex-roadie who owned the joint, was as cool as they came.

No, the actual problem of Hoo Hah's was that it was just that. Hoo Hah's. And in two years time, it was still a staple in Narwhal's short list of gigs. The greatest improvement the members of Narwhal had achieved was the fact that they were now playing after shitty pop-punk bands with dumbass names like Lost Baggage instead of before them.

But still, they were yet to be an alpha male like Alpha Male, who they had opened for tonight. A local band, just like Johnny and his friends, but who had somehow made one of their tracks the fight song for the city's hockey team. Eddie had said: "Fuck that shit, man. Do you really want our fan base to be a bunch of frat boys and rich bitches? Alpha Male is poser shit."

A valid point. An accurate statement. But Alpha Male had just been signed by Capitol to release their first album, *A.M. Radio*. If that was the payoff, Johnny would have gladly written the theme song for a Big Bang Theory spin-off show. But Roger was right about one thing: Alpha Male sucked. Johnny threw a five on the bar and clumsily slid off his stool. Marty came walking over to collect the tab.

"Great set tonight, man. As always."

Johnny finished the last swig of his drink. "Thank you, sir. And it always means a lot coming from you." He then handed the owner/bartender his glass. "And we will be seeing you in two weeks if I'm not mistaken."

Marty nodded his head in affirmation. "Yup, the sixteenth. And let me just say I'm honored you chose my place to be your last show."

Up on stage, Alpha Male was busy jamming away and the speakers were cranked to the max. Surely, Johnny had heard Marty wrong. "What was that?"

"I said it sucks that you're leaving the band, but I'm proud to say the last Narwhal show was performed on my stage. Or, at least as far as I'm concerned, the last *true* Narwhal show."

Johnny could feel that his face was frozen in a rather peculiar open-mouthed smirk. "How did you hear that?" he asked as casually as possible.

Marty was being flagged by a customer down the bar and answered as he walked away. "Eddie told me when you were helping Buzz set up his drumkit. Honestly, I think you guys work better as a trio, but I understand with guitar and drum duos being so hot right now. But best of luck to you with your new band!"

The last part was shouted as Marty put up one hand to wave goodbye. Johnny returned the gesture and spun around, hardly feeling the effects of the alcohol but dazed nonetheless. After years of playing in crammed clubs and bars, Johnny had long ago adapted to the high temperatures of such environments. But as he made his way to the exit, the apparent ex-bassist of Narwhal was feeling hotter than he'd ever felt before. A fever of hate burned behind his ears. Another blazed in his belly.

So Eddie wanted to be Jack fucking White: center stage, both singing and shredding, and practically alone in the spotlight. Not including, of course, a drummer who wanted to ride Eddie's "talent" while he banged away like a wind-up chimp behind his guitarist's shadow. Through the whites and reds and yellows of his anger, Johnny could faintly see glimpses of why this made sense. Eddie wanted more stage, plain and simple. Probably did from the very conception of Narwhal when they were originally called *The* Narwhals. But Roger was around back then, the obvious best choice for front man, so Eddie had to go with it.

But just like that, in a drunk driving accident, Roger died. As the former backing vocalist, the mic was handed to Johnny and again, Eddie was on the far right of the stage. But convince the drummer that you can sing just as well and that there are plenty of successful bands out there without bassists...and look what happens.

A part of Johnny admired Eddie for his strategy. He saw an opportunity to get what he wanted and was taking it. And with a two-to-one vote, what could Johnny do?

But then again, Eddie and Buzz were giving Johnny one last show. One last hoorah at Hoo Hah's. There was still time. He wasn't out of the band yet.

It had been a close call. Even with the extra money Johnny had spent on expedited shipping, it was always hard to say how fast something shipped from Zambia would reach the United States. But with only one remaining day until the big show, Johnny returned to his apartment to find a large wooden box waiting for him by the front door.

Several stamps and stickers had been adhered to all sides of the box during its long journey, practically obscuring Johnny's address. Nevertheless, the postal service had known where to bring this oversized package and Johnny almost couldn't contain his excitement as he heaved it over the threshold into his abode. Two days prior, Johnny had lifted a crowbar from the foundry where he worked making metal castings. It was a shit job that paid him in peanuts, so Johnny had no qualms about stealing one little crowbar from his asshole foreman. Grabbing the tool from his kitchen counter, Johnny went to work prying the box apart. Wood splintered and sawdust fell like snow to the carpet as the box slowly but surely gave way. Finally, after all necessary nails had been lifted and all packaging tape torn, the prize within was revealed.

A new bass guitar.

At first glance, the bass seemed to be your standard cliché death metal machine. The case, not accidentally coffin shaped, a beautiful construction of polished oak, had been painted black. Dark purple velvet lined the inside, padding it as if it were meant for human remains and not an instrument. And if the website in which Johnny had discovered his purchase had published the truth, that's exactly what this case originally had been: a coffin for a young African boy.

After the appropriate amount of admiration was shown towards the outer shell, Johnny opened it to reveal the bass itself. If hung as an exhibit it would have appeared a ghastly thing to anyone passing by. But to Johnny, it was nothing short of beautiful; nothing short of perfect.

There was no telling what material had been fashioned to make the neck, for it was wrapped in real snakeskin, perfectly preserved. Even the snake's head was intact, complimenting the headstock with a vicious frozen stare, mouth gaping, fangs and all. Slightly below the snake's eyes (which had been replaced with green stones, perhaps jade), ebony tuning knobs protruded from both sides.

The bass's body had been crafted to resemble a human hand, palm up. Five sculpted fingers curled upward to create the appearance that the guitar could actually hold something if an object was placed within. The fingers were inhuman, extraordinarily long with black talons in place of fingernails. In the center, where the strings were to be strummed, picked, or slapped, an ivory eyeball with painted bloodshot stared at nothing yet met your gaze no matter how you turned the bass in your hands.

Even without the promise that the vibrations created by playing the bass's strings could be felt by the deceased buried six feet under, Johnny was proud to be its owner. Those were just exaggerations anyhow, marketing gimmicks to sell more guitars. It was just a classic rock and roll saying. "It's loud enough to wake the dead." But that metaphor didn't really claim importance here. All Johnny wanted was an axe that would catch anyone's attention who happened to glance at the stage. A bass so kick-ass that one couldn't tear their eyes from it, no matter how amazingly Eddie might perform. This bass was a scene-stealer, a showstopper, a thunder-thief. And as Johnny looked his new possession up and down and up again, he couldn't wipe the grin from his face. In his skilled hands, this bass would be unstoppable. No one would care about anything else.

Johnny counted off.

"One, two, three, four!"

And Narwhal's show was underway with an opening cover of "Blitzkreig Bop." The crowd cheered in response to the familiar noise. And as Johnny began to sing the first lines of the song, he noticed what he had come to expect: everyone was staring at his instrument. No matter how much enthusiasm or showmanship Eddie displayed, the crowd could not turn away. The giant eye of Johnny's guitar continued to hold their gaze, even if Buzz erupted in the most massive drumming explosion. They cheered, they clapped, but they didn't seem to blink. And Johnny could tell that Eddie was pissed. This couldn't get any better.

But then about halfway through their show, it somehow did. At first Johnny hadn't noticed, too caught up in the moment, feeling his reputation grow with every passing minute. Gradually, though, it became too obvious to ignore. The crowd was growing. A lot. Hoo Hah's wasn't a big place to begin with so it always seemed crowded no matter what, but this was absurd. During a break in the lyrics, Johnny craned his neck to see over the audience and caught a glimpse of a current of people coming in through the front entrance.

Why wasn't the bouncer stopping them? Johnny was more than happy to play for the entire world if they so desired, but didn't Marty have to follow some kind of fire code? They had to be way past their maximum allowed capacity of attendees. But although Johnny could clearly see the bar from high up on stage, Marty was nowhere in sight. Well, whatever, Johnny thought. It wasn't his problem. As far as he was concerned, the more the merrier, and he continued to play even harder. The crowd continued to stare.

It was moments before Johnny was about to let loose a voice cracking wail when he realized Buzz was no longer playing. Assuming it was a mere case of a dropped stick, Johnny inhaled deeply getting ready to release his scream. But Buzz still wasn't playing and Johnny couldn't help but turn around.

Buzz was no longer sitting at his set but standing very erect and looking down at the front row. Maybe someone had thrown a beer can or done something to his drummer to deserve retaliation.

When Johnny spun around to determine whatever was causing such an interruption, Eddie stopped playing as well. Now only Johnny plucked on, and oddly, the audience's reaction was exactly the same: staring straight ahead as if in a trance.

"What the fuck?" Eddie shouted, appalled.

By following Eddie's line of sight, Johnny finally saw what had stopped both his drummer and guitarist in mid-song. An audience member was ripping open the throat of the man next to him. Johnny's hands continued to play of their own accord, his mind completely separate from his body. It seemed no one in the crowd was paying any attention to the ultra-violence, ignoring the spurting blood and severed arteries as if it was all just another harmless shove of a typical mosh pit. But what shocked Johnny most of all was that the victim himself wasn't reacting in the slightest. He was only staring straight ahead at Johnny's bass, unblinking even as his Adam's apple was exposed.

Now the spell of his creative flow was totally broken and Johnny was fully observing his surroundings for the first time. He saw that the man sinking his teeth into another's throat was not a solitary occurrence. Bloody bodies were scattered among the feet of those still standing. A massacre had occurred during Narwhal's set and Johnny, so enveloped in his performance and blinded by stage lights, hadn't even noticed.

It took the sudden appearance of Marty's severed head sitting on a bar stool to finally make Johnny stop playing. His finger slipped on a D note and the room was as silent as death.

Then the crowd began shuffling forward.

Eddie tripped over a cord as he darted backward. Buzz knocked over his high-hat as he frantically looked for a way off the stage. They were absolutely terrified of the faces that approached them: glassy, lifeless eyes. Green, decaying skin. Dirt, maggots, and congealing blood smeared their mouths. This was the crowd of the dead. And the crowd had turned on their performers like (and yet very unlike) so many crowds before.

However, Johnny did not join his bandmates in their pathetic huddle at the rear of the stage. He paid no mind to the zombie hordes that were trying to figure out how to climb up to the band's level. Johnny was staring past them towards the bar, the far end to be exact. Only a solitary barstool was occupied. He was undead, like the rest, woken by the vibrations of Johnny's new voodoo bass.

But he was different. Johnny recognized him, even with the patches of flesh missing and moss clinging to his bones.

Roger raised a glass of whiskey and grinned. Just as the horde had discovered how to pile themselves high enough to reach their prey, Roger placed the glass on the counter and mimicked a familiar motion: fingering a bass. Johnny complied with his dead friend's wishes and plucked a string.

And just like that the crowd froze. Johnny hit another note. They started bacwards. Another note, then another, and "Number of the Beast" radiated from the house speakers. The crowd erupted in what couldn't be called cheers, but cheerful moans. Roger flashed Johnny a thumb's up.

It was more than enough support Johnny needed. He turned to his bandmates, who were shivering and the on verge of tears.

"C'mon, you guys, they love us! Let's hit it!"

Eddie and Buzz remained still. Johnny snarled. "Let me hear you or I'll stop!"

In an instant, Buzz retrieved his sticks and found the beat. Eddie replaced the strap of his guitar to his shoulder and immediately joined in. The two looked terrified. Tormented. Tortured.

But Johnny was happy. He had never known such satisfaction, and it warmed him like alcohol. He'd finally found an audience who listened. Who only cared about those sweet, deep vibes coming from his fingers. Johnny was the most important person on stage. Hell, to these rotting faces and dead stares, Johnny was the only person who mattered on Earth. And how different it all felt.

Because no one ever really listens to the bass. Just like Johnny, the bass had been taken for granted, assumed to always be there in the background. But you take the bass away, and all of a sudden…people notice.

Johnny turned his wide-eyed gaze from the crowd to meet Eddie's expression of total fright. He turned back to Buzz and saw an identical look of fear.

Johnny grinned, ecstatic and insane. Oh yes. If he stopped playing, they would notice.

THE BASEMENT PEOPLE

BY NICHOLAUS PATNAUDE

THE RATTLER, November 16th, 1981: THE BASEMENT PEOPLE RELEASED ON $50,000 BOND – BASEMENT PEOPLE IN WASHING MACHINE HAVING ORGY DURING MURDER OF DEBORAH WEISS. "The conjoined conglomeration of hairy human and inhuman limbs – the self-described post-punk group The Basement People – were released on $50,000 bond this morning. They are accused of murdering Deborah Weiss. 'We don't know what happened. We were just minding our own business and having an orgy in the washing machine when Deborah was killed,' The Basement People stated. When asked how Deborah subsequently transformed into a zombie, The Basement People retreated into their cloud of swinging limbs and drifted up into the sky without answering."

BOBBY BANG BANG DRACULA: Reb and I were friends. Sure. We go way back. I remember him dead-broke singing for pennies in Wishbone Alley before the money started coming in. I was there the night all the shit went down. A lot of it's blocked out, though. Scrambled. I just have some scattered images is all, lasered to my fucking retinas. I remember Reb backing into a corner of his penthouse suite, the gooey yellow shadows of zombie virus pulsing forward. He said something like: "Just draw a picture of a washing machine on the wall like you did before. Walk backward into it to join the Basement People." I'm not sure who he was talking to. Himself? Deborah? The Basement People? Another strange thing about that night was how Deborah got trapped in the party. She was somehow subsumed in the event itself. Her hair, her skin, her mind. All trapped within the fractions of party time, like butter leaking off toast into the coils of a toaster.

A CURSED PAIR OF GO-GO BOOTS: The zombie virus had already overtaken Deborah a few weeks before the party in which she got forever lost. She sat up, her purple mohawk glinting like a spinning saw from all the extra wax Reb had painstakingly applied while repeating, "you were a rebel in life. Why not be a rebel in death too?" She drooled. Soon, she would wake completely. *A zombie in life and a zombie in death.* That was the cruel maxim Reb would repeat during those lonely weeks when music was his only companion. After the Deborah he loved had disappeared into the party, Reb smoked as many cigarettes as Ian Curtis. We peered at him from beneath the bed; he'd tossed us beside cowboy boots and combat boots – strange that he would treat go-go boots so rudely! Especially when go-go boots as a symbol to the Dirtywater post-punk scene are as important as that block of ice beneath Ian Curtis when he hung himself with barb wire.

NIKKI COLD WAVE: That was the thing about Deborah: she always chose to partake in a smaller rebellion and missed out on a much grander rebellion. At least this is what Reb told us to believe. And he allowed the Basement People to appear in our skulls. They chatter. We listen. Forever adhere to the beloved brotherhood of our holy Basement People. She died her hair blue, pierced her face with railroad spikes, listened to anarchic crusty punk like Discharge, but she never rebelled against existence itself. Didn't she ever consider loving and then rebelling against death? I'd ask her stuff like this every day, but Deborah would just continue to drool – she'd been transformed into a zombie by this point. This was a few days after she'd gotten lost within that infamous party. Her unblinking eyes had turned to hollow caverns; a thin piano would play faintly like at the beginning of "Who Killed Mr. Moonlight," beckoning one to wander down their empty hallways and disappear. I was tempted too. And every time the Basement People would be there waiting.

ZOMBIE REB: Don't let the 12 ice versions of yourself that were just onstage fool anyone. That's something I'd tell myself after my performances would begin. It was tricky not to take part in one's own performances, but, somehow, I managed. Thanks to the Basement People.

BRIDGET LAYHAY: The Basement People would rise, but Reb prayed post-punk was just beginning. Post-punk was the spirit without the scrambling adolescent fury of punk; post-punk was an emanation of the cold cruelty he'd always felt inside, fossilizing like cursed dinosaur bones deep beneath a wintry forest; post-punk was an approximation of his warped outlook – a psychological state scrambled by an alien being, crystallized on vinyl. At least that's how he'd put it in interviews. He'd shaved off his spiked hair and removed his lock and chain necklace more than a month before Deborah fell through the cracks of the party. Donning a black and white suit with a thin black tie wasn't a bold statement in the scene, but adding spurred cowboy boots and shark tooth earrings was! Made him look like he belonged alongside strung-out Nick Cave screaming while swaying and channeling his demons. A long lost member of the Birthday Party. Punk died because it needed to evolve, like a suicidal Tyrannosaurs Rex in an ocean of its own tears. That was another one of Reb's odd but unforgettable maxims.

BOBBY BANG BANG DRACULA: A lot of us in Dirtywater were obsessed with *Burning from the Inside* and early noise records, mostly Blind Owl EPs and Psychedelic Pornography compilations. Reb lowered the needle on *Burning From the Inside* for the fourth or fifth time that evening, I remember. A life-size puppet of Deborah sat beside her zombie version. Flies crawled on each version's cheeks. Reb howled along with Peter Murphy on Antonin Artaud as he swiveled in his chair past the ten black and white monitors. Images of the residents in his apartment complex were reflected in his pale blue eyes. He certainly had a magic power over them all. They were his kittens, as he liked to refer to them. The way they played their games, lived their lives, was funny to Reb. One time he started chanting that eerie last part on Antonin Artaud about Indians cumming on their own bones when it was just the two of us sixty-nining in bed. He'd cover that song at the end of every show-- – he'd get so wild and frenzied that the crowd would start crying along about Indians wanking on bones. He was a sick bastard, but I sure as fuck loved him. Yeah, even after he became a fucking zombie.

TROMBONE COCK WEASEL: "Deborah, I caught you laughing. I caught you. I recorded you. I could watch you in slow motion forever." Those were the exact words I remember Reb saying on the night in question. There was supposed to have been a party at his place. He cancelled it, but people came anyway. I think the theme was Underwater Death or something because everyone dressed as bright dead fish leaking weird colored blood. Then he let some of us hang around to "see inside his private display case" as he'd put it. I don't want to talk about what we saw inside of there, but I will say that crimes themselves are capable of mutating.

BRIDGET LAYHAY: A pale blue ghost version of Deborah wavered like a candle flame between her motionless zombie form and her puppet version, the latter of which eagerly ate ants off her cheeks. That was what we saw inside his display case – an enormous, empty fish tank, the sort of tank you'd keep a pet anaconda in.

Plumes of brown smoke rose from the stovetop. Oblivious to the burning smell, Reb placed an ice version of himself next to each black and white television monitor. The ice versions of himself that used to perform in the clubs. A private moment of each tenant. He sucked in these secrets like a ghoulish addict.

Needing a break from the tension in the room, I went up to the roof for a cigarette. Wind formed into a tall, thin man. He called himself Mr. Moonlight. Mr. Moonlight wore a cap with lightning bolt patterns and a gray woolen coat. Blasts of snow furiously fell as he waddled downstairs.

NIKKI COLDWAVE: Mr. Moonlight's gaunt shadow was as imposing as Ian Curtis's. Fumes escaped from beneath the wings on his cap. He drifted down the stairs from the roof; that's the story I heard. His shadow somersaulted and twisted on the stairwell walls. Dials in his eyes spun ruthlessly. He rang Reb's doorbell. His chrome lips curled into a fiendish smile, emulating human congeniality.

BOBBY BANG BANG DRACULA: You used to be able to get the best key lime pie at a shop near Reb's place. They had stained glass windows for doors, Formica tabletops, and loads of photographs of Elvis fucking Marylyn Monroe. The party was the same day Reb stole some of those pictures – his prize was one of the king fisting Kennedy's hot side project; the king was elbow-deep and the queen had her curls thrown back like he was the funniest court jester in all the land. I remember we were inter-rupted. Reb had his hand down my jeans getting me wild, but the knock killed the mood, which was unfortunate since I was twice as turned on by everybody watching us. Reb peered through the peephole, but Mr. Moonlight knew better for his purposes than to stand in front of it. Wires detached from his lips like octopus tentacles. One pierced through the peephole and deposited an injection directly into Reb's pupil. And just like that my lover changed forever.

A PAIR OF CURSED GO-GO BOOTS: The party got insane later that night. Reb obeyed "the throbbing command." He opened the door to his immaculate penthouse apartment for Mr. Moonlight. Sparsely furnished, an odd sculpture resembling a blurred part of the human body on pedestals were here and there, mostly in the corners. The floor was white marble. Gold insect figurines were attached to the ceiling, their precious gem ears and eyes glittering in the half-light. We begged Reb to wear us but he's never been able to hear our language.

BRIDGET LAYHAY: Mr. Moonlight was a total creep. He spoke in this robotic voice. "I want to form a band with you. For your part, you must play the cinderblocks with a hammer." He somehow removed cinderblocks from his coat pocket and stacked them irregularly around Reb. Then he handed hammers to Reb for drumsticks and tinkered with a mini analog synthe-sizer in his coat pocket. This was way before we started the Licorice Sisters, back when JamTrax and Colder Than Thou's Alien Soul were actually releasing experimental EPs. Then he said, "For the singer, we will use the zombies." He curled a finger and leered with his chrome jaw as he beckoned the three Debo-rahs – the zombie, the ghost, and the puppet. "Our name will be The Basement People," Mr. Moonlight said with a faint German accent. But there was already another group named the Basement People, and they weren't exactly human.

A PAIR OF CURSED GO-GO BOOTS: The Basement people tittered in their lair, giggling and growling hysterically at the prospect of violence. They'd already killed so many stuffed animals the day of the party for their rituals. They jumped together from their basement tree house like a pack of lemmings leaping and burning into a fuming cloud, landing in The Rabid Sea, a puddle beside the washing machine. They multiplied. Stray legs burst from the cloud of hybrid limbs and skeletal faces and flexed with new muscles at every mention of their name. Spark fleas – a species they'd harvested from the Rabid Sea – were already springing from hide to hide among The Basement People, creating living currents of electricity. When Deborah wore us for a twenty mile hike around in circles in their basement lair, they tried to infest us. They were like a contagious disease. or a mold always lurking within the apartment complex, ready to reemerge the moment we let our guards down.

BOBBY BANG BANG DRACULA: Zombie Deborah, Puppet Deborah, and Ghost Deborah all leaned into the microphones and sang. Reb kept a consistent beat on the cinderblocks with the hammers while Mr. Moonlight stirred up eerie sound textures on the synthesizer. He turned the knobs and unplugged wires with a fiendish pace. "From the riverssssss of my lunnnnnngs, I need to tell you all about how my lover killllllllled meeeeeeeee," the zombie Deborah began.

A CURSED PAIR OF GO-GO BOOTS: The pair of sprites animating us had recently expired, so we were waiting for a new ghoul to take us over and posses our soles. We so wanted to slide up and hug Deborah's smooth legs. Down below, The Basement People threw the underwear of the tenants back and forth from washing machine to washing machine, their furry hamster skin glistening. Muscles flexed beneath mounds and mounds of fur. They listened avidly to the song, pressing their pointed ears against the pipes leading to Reb's penthouse apartment.

GHOST DEBORAH: I was once a tenant in this building. I only wanted to make paintings. I'd already sold a couple to a few post-punk bands. Mainly black and white paintings of crumbling statues, similar to the art on The Damned's *Phantasmagoria 2* LP. A few other post-punk bands had used them as flyers. Obscure Factory Records stuff. You probably haven't heard of them.

One night I was relaxing in my bedroom. I lived alone, but I needed someone that night. I felt relaxed. I remember the raindrops on my windowpane. I ran a finger down my silk stocking.

I imagined smashing the lead singer of Teasy Robo's jaw with a wrench. I shuddered. The rain became cool green poison. Mice scurrying in the walls. Teasy Robo would swing his wild greasy hair, eager to destroy an instrument or get a bottle thrown at his head. Sometimes he reminded me of Darby Crash. I wanted to take a knife to his throat. Force him to kink his back until it broke and he sucked himself. Hot white cum would leak down his chin as I pumped him full of the electric bolts darting from my eyes. I started to touch myself then. Clean circles. Ripping shear panties. Blood on a doily. Soaking through layers of silk. Your lips pressed too hard against an edible insect. I needed something nasty to keep me interested. I want to be sex positive, but that just isn't what turns me on.

I closed and clouded my eyes, establishing a nice little in and out rhythm of slick jilling sounds, spreading myself like a fan as my fingers darted in and out. Terrified worms spasming. My inner thighs quaking with lightning bolts. Then I heard an electric gizmo. It had come from the fire alarm. A video camera behind it zoomed in and out.

THE BASEMENT PEOPLE: Debrorah's body flickered in and out like a projection. She sighed. While adjusting her skull blouse, her pale blue skin looked purplish under the dying light bulbs. Menstrual blood streamed down her thighs. It was time to bite off Reb's cock again and again until he flickered out of existence. Blood poured from above his eye. His calf throbbed from a strain after walking around and around the Rabid Sea in our basement lair for twenty miles.

GHOST DEBORAH: Furious about being spied on, I called the landlord. Reb answered on the first ring. He was outraged that someone would do this – spy on me. At least he pretended to be. He told me to come to his penthouse apartment immediately so we could get to the bottom of this. He had to buzz me up because the elevator opened directly into his apartment. I remember that all the lights were off, yet these gold insects he had scattered on columns and pedestals glowed with a bluish light. He came out of nowhere, slicing into my spine with a kitchen knife. As I lay paralyzed on the floor, his lips covered in my blood, he proceeded to push my menstrual blood-stained panties toward my face. But I let the animal out, gnashed up his cheeks, and strangled him instead, yet the crime kept changing as we tumbled and fought just like we had become our own jumbled mass of hairy limbs like The Basement People. The crime mutated. First I'd bite off his cock and choke him with it, then it'd grow back and he'd have the upper hand, choking me with my panties or he'd be strangling me with them. As I've stated a thousand times before on record, the crime itself kept changing. Our corpses – we were both killed by the simultaneous, though opposite, crimes – have been rotting here ever since, until we became zombies, that is. Are you even ready for that part of the story, though?

BOBBY BANG BANG DRACULA: Mr. Moonlight abruptly stopped playing the synthesizer.

Beads of sweat poured down Reb's forehead.

The Basement People rose up out of the marble floor. Squatting like rodents, their shocks of hair standing on end, their faces lively but skeletal.

ZOMBIE REB: She's lying. *Lying.* I didn't do any of that. Or maybe I did, but on a different timeline. Even Deborah agrees that the crime kept mutating, which means neither of us really did anything illegal. It was the Basement People. Somehow, they were controlling the mutations of the crime. And look at me now? I'm useless. *I'm a fucking drooling zombie!*

BRIDGET LAYHAY: Although zombie Reb had merely meant to tap zombie Deborah lightly with a hammer, he knocked off her head with a single swipe. It rolled over to the Basement People.

A hairy one with a human baby body lifted her head and took a fist-sized bite out of it. "So this is our lunch then." The Basement People tittered. The zombie virus ran rampantly through the veins of all The Basement People, then cleanly exited their bloodstreams in a serpentine rush of yellow light.

"We are the Basement People." They kept repeating that. The throng of human skeleton and rodent hybrids rushed back and forth across the room. Only a miniature cowboy could corral them into a herd. Some held raging comets attached to strings, like balloons. Others mimicked the grinning faces of ghouls and goblins.

The zombie virus surged through the air, assuming a demonic form – an angel of death fashioned from electricity and sparking yellow light, ready to pounce on its next victim.

NIKKI COLDWAVE: "Look, we want to bestow upon you the

zombie virus," Mr. Moonlight, still wearing the winged hat and the long woolen coat, began. "But we would first like you to answer for your accusations. Did you, Reb Jensen, strangle this decapitated zombie girl named Deborah with her own panties? Or did she sever your penis and then choke you with it?" The silver wings on his cap fluttered and rose a few inches off the ground. His chrome jaw gleamed, assuming an expression of consternation and silent judgment.

ZOMBIE REB: Will you at least listen to my version of the events?

A CURSED PAIR OF GO-GO BOOTS: The Basement People became hysterical, hopping about the room gymnastically, engaging in a gruesome battle and an orgy simultaneously, mostly obscured from view by smoke, tufts of fur, and faint flash-ings of light like lightning obscured by blankets of cloud. "We are the Basement People. *We are the Basement People.*" Sure they were brutish, but at least they were enthusiastic.

ZOMBIE DEBORAH: I was on the way home from a Bauhaus concert. It was the first time I'd ever seen them. It was during their *Burning From the Inside* tour. I slipped and hit my head on my marble floor after I came back to my apartment. The Base-ment People were there that night. They were the size of fleas. Glowing, they hovered around me like hairy lightning bugs – this was well before their legendary growth spurt – yet their twitching rodent and reptile eyes stared back through human skulls. Laughing in their high-pitch squeal, they helped me up while infesting my brain.

ZOMBIE DEBORAH: You pushed my panties past my teeth. I jammed your cock past your teeth. Your thumb smelled of turpentine when you jammed up my nose to stop me. My fingers smelled of menstrual blood when I lost all sense of mercy and blocked the oxygen to your brain. Reb ate my brain. I ate my brain. I hate Reb's brain. Together, we ate the zombie rain.

ZOMBIE REB: I went to my inner chamber *merely to observe* the inhabitants of my apartment complex like a Batman or a Superman—I admire how they look after their citizens in case they encounter any danger, but of course *she had to tempt me.* Burrowing her fingers into that little nub of pink flesh, stretching and pulling at the hairs. Opening that little mouth wider and wider, as if it could speak to me. As if it wanted to smother me.

More hungry than any other mouth. The hairy flesh shaking as if delightful doors were opening, each layer more joyous, and a lighter shade of pink, than the last.

PUPPET DEBORAH: I beat Reb's dead body with a baseball bat. Pieces of my teeth fell through my fingers. I ground and ground them in a mad blood rage to powdery flakes. Sorry. Ever since I lost my teeth, I have trouble speaking. I wish my lips were stitched shut.

ZOMBIE REB: The others in the video monitors told me to do it. *They encouraged me. The Basement People were with me.* Don't you guys remember? After she broke my back, I could suck my own cock. It was glorious! But too glorious, as it turned out. I bit the damn thing clean off and choked *myself* to death. That was the part she always got wrong, even when considering the mutability of the crime itself. I never laid a hand *on her*.

A CURSED PAIR OF GO-GO BOOTS: "We are The Basement People," the herd of hairy limbs and skeleton faces shouted. The zombie virus drifted overhead in the shape of a beautiful hermaphrodite, contemplating who next to infest, its skin jagged with yellow electrical currents, its high cheekbones adhering to Renaissance artist golden ratio rules with exactitude – in other words, the virus looked like a fucking god.

AN ELDERLY WOMAN SWEEPING HER KITCHEN IN ONE OF REB'S VIDEO MONITORS: Thanks for watching over us. I just love being spied upon. You did a good thing by murdering that girl Deborah. And she did good by murdering you too! And by asphyxiation via your own schlong to boot! Now that takes class! She once baked me a blueberry pie. Another time – back when I was drinking – she drove my son Paul to the hospital after he cut off his finger. Serves her right!

AN ELDERLY MAN WHITTLING ON HIS BALCONY IN A VIDEO MONITOR: She sewed me a delightful evening gown which I wore to my Tool and Dye company's crystal ball. She also used to bake me snicker doodles, so it makes sense that you violated her after you savagely murdered her with your bare hands or that she rammed your own johnson down your throat until you kicked the bucket, depending on which form of the crime happens to exist at any given moment, that is. Thanks! You really did us all a favor!

ANOTHER ELDERLY WOMAN SMOKING IN A VIDEO

MONITOR: Deborah went ahead and walked foolishly into that panty-strangling trap? You don't say! She used to deliver fresh fruit to me and do all of my grocery shopping. Thank you for killing her and for spying on me all these years! You're my knight! My beacon of hope! My savior! Great to hear that you got a taste of your own panty-strangling medicine too when she went ahead and shimmied your one-eyed snake down your puke pipe when the crime itself chose to mutate. That girl had grit! Was it worth it? Hey buddy, you ever want to ramble down this cobwebbed snatch cavern you give me a call. I'll even eat your brains for free afterward.

ZOMBIE REB: See what I mean?

THE BASEMENT PEOPLE: See what he means? Means what he sees? Meanie see, meanie do!

A CURSED PAIR OF GO-GO BOOTS: The Basement People chanted and chatted. One skull-faced person with raccoon fur jumped out of the smoky, floating menagerie of orgy and war as if there were a trampoline inside that misty, enchanted mass.

THE BASEMENT PEOPLE: He's Prince Innocent. And I think I'm in love. L-U-V. We feel freezing. We drink the dew from the fruit trees in the basement. We drink trees from this basement earth. We realize the beauty of the oily water leaking from the washing machine. We eat bones alive. We live between the cracking of the finger joints in the cracking of the seconds.

ZOMBIE REB: Therefore, I accepted the zombie virus into my heart. To and to hold forever and ever. Amen. I kneeled, crossed myself, and prayed.

BOBBY BANG BANG DRACULA: Mr. Moonlight guided the zombie virus down Reb's throat. Reb foamed at the mouth. He shook. His limbs twisted. Finally, he collapsed while convulsing.

A CURSED PAIR OF GO-GO BOOTS: The Basement People cheered. So did all the tenants staring out of the black and white video monitors. Our soles purred in delight.

BRIDGET LAYHAY: The transformation was complete. Reb lurched over to the turntable. Although he removed the vinyl from the record sleeve too quickly to be seen, we all knew which record he'd chosen.

"She's in Parties" escaped from Peter Murphy's trapped lips within the vinyl grooves. Guitar tones emulating clean, compact saws followed. The Basement People danced and danced until the marble floor eroded beneath their hundreds of hooves, claws, and skeletal toes. They fell through the floor of each apartment below Reb's, dancing and dancing to some inner devil until all the other tenants could also spy on Reb 24 hours a day and appreciate the private life of their zombie savior.

THE RATTLER, NOVEMBER 20TH, 1983: COURT PLAGUED BY ZOMBIE VIRUS – WILL JUDGE EVER RETURN FROM SWARM OF BASEMENT PEOPLE? "Judge Jimmy Booker disappeared into the swarm of human, rodent, and baby limbs when he purportedly went into a trance and wandered into a smoky cloud where both a fight and an orgy occurred simultaneously. Before ultimately disappearing, several witnesses stated Booked said, 'I deem you guilty as charged, but we are The Basement People. Never follow your dreams to our spiraling hallways. Follow your demons to the forest at the edge of the green desert. Horse heads float in a lake there. *Talk to them. Tell them your horrible feelings before it's too late*. We are the Basement People. *We* are the Basement People.'"

NATURE UNVEILED

BY SAM RICHARD

I buried her ashes in a salt urn at the crux of two rivers, deep into the sand at low tide, as one should do with a witch of such immense power. I could feel the weight of her ashes, heavy in my hands, heavy in my head, heavy in my heart. She once told me that the greatest gift one could give was to return back to nature, as we had all taken so much. She also told me that some people took too much, and never gave back, so maybe nature should have a little help doing the job.

Obviously, I never imagined it would happen this soon, as one never does with young death. I imagined myself straining with the back of an 80 year old, knees cracking, joints burning, trying to accomplish her life's final ritual fuck you. Or, to truly be honest, I pictured that I'd be the first to die. That she would be the one doing the digging with salt-chapped eyes, trying to figure out how to carry on. Not me, on my knees at 35, tired and worn and wounded and lost. It certainly isn't 80, with a long life behind us. No, it's 35, with 5 years behind us – 5 fucking incredible years – and a bleak lifetime without her ahead.

When we met she had already begun her life's ritual working. She had dark, close-cropped hair and looked like a French model from the 1960s, ever an American Spirit between two fingers and the hoppiest beer available casually held in her other hand. We shared esoteric secrets that first night; we unveiled the cosmos and poured its illuminating darkness into our feeble minds. It changed us. We changed us. Not gods, not magick, not theology or psychology. No, we were the ritual. We were the great work.

After six months, she moved in with me. Well, us. It was a standard rotting punk house, complete with a smelly, adorable dog and an even smellier, not adorable, roommate. We did our best to spice up the place, to make it a home for both of us. It was important to me that she didn't just cram her belongings into my space. She later said that she was impressed that I had a nice couch, a bedroom full of books, and a decent record collection. The last guy she had dated lived in a garage and had a psychotic break. Apparently, I was quite the step up.

At night we created together, me writing, and her making art. I was working on a horror novel about the wounds that religion inflicts and how to burn down your local church, while she was creating her own tarot deck, along with all the drawing that accompanies being a tattoo artist. Her deck featured nature as the main theme; the cards were colorful and vibrant, even shimmering at times. She researched the convoluted history of the tarot, soaking bits of knowledge into her brain like a sponge.

Occasionally, we would slink to the basement and work on music together. She played bass with all that hyper-cool, repetitive post-punk rumbling; I played guitar, trying my best to blend post-punk and neo-folk; dark, morose melodies, murder ballads, and a reverb-drenched wall. We shared vocals, and a cheap 90s drum machine did the rest. It wasn't much, but it was what we could make together. We released a few demos and played a handful of shows; basements that sweat down the walls with the moisture of too many people in a small space on a hot night.

She cut images into people's skin while I slaved away in the kitchen of a shitty vegan restaurant. Eventually, all her hard work paid off, and we were able to move away from the smelly dog and his smellier owner. We got our own dog, Caligula, and our own place. We built a life and, somewhere along the way, our rituals collided and became intermingled with every fiber of that life. As we lived our disbelief, we also lived our malleable beliefs when they suited us, and discarded them when they didn't. As we lived our discontent with the horrors of the world, we also live our contentment with the life we were creating together.

We would bitch about the many luxury condos gentrifying the city, and before we knew it, a quarter of them had mysteriously burned to the ground. At first, we didn't think we were responsible. How could that have even been possible? But it kept happening. So we tried to focus this phenomenon, to test it, like a lab experiment – the aim of religion with the rigor of science, right? Fancy headwear stores, chain restaurants, and upscale gluten-free bakeries all fell under our power. At least we hoped they did; maybe they were just bad at business.

We re-read Burroughs and Gysin, P-Orridge, Hine, Carrol, Morrison, Spare, and Parsons. The Burroughs/Gysin experiments became like a bible to us. We called upon the Third Mind, met our Holy Guardian Angels, and Undid Ourselves. We re-examined Crowley, Dee, Abramelin, and Agrippa, and twisted them into the post-post-modern landscape, taking what we needed and burning the rest. Our insurrection came under the guise of the esoteric, and our disbelief came under the guise of belief. Our love for each other was our god and the natural world was our temple, but we couldn't just retreat into it all like hermits; we needed to bring action to our disbelief. We were a two person Up Against the Wall Motherfucker, with heads full of the Western Esoteric Tradition, and hearts full of fire.

We thought bigger – banking and finance, religion, politics, government, worldwide neo-liberal economic systems, institutional racism. They were harder, protected, fortified. Like the oldest forms of magick, built and maintained by a legacy of misery. These were ancient, ugly forces and they were protected with strength that I could never have conceived possible. By the time we realized that we had gone too deep, it was far too late.

I got sick. It felt like there were parasites that attached to me. It's hard to explain and I don't really know if I believed that this was something that was possible, but I found myself increasingly drained and exhausted. My mind was flooded with horrifying visions of my deepest fears, all manner of horrifying creature and concept taken from my oldest, darkest memories. Sleep became elusive as life felt like a fever dream. Or maybe I was just paranoid, ill.

I'd like to say that "They" did something to her. It would

make it all so much easier if she died because of some mysterious Cabal of "Them," but she didn't; "They" didn't. One day she went to work and within a couple hours she had collapsed, dead the moment she hit the ground. The doctors said it was an aortic aneurysm, that her heart had exploded. Here and then gone. There was nothing that they could do. Shock and awe are only words. Sorrow is only a word. Grief is only a word. Words are symbols meant to make abstract concepts housebroken. The truths lying beneath sorrow, grief, are so much worse than anything I could ever conjure on my own.

She didn't want anything fancy, just that we would celebrate her life. Family, friends, and clients filled the small chapel where her memorial service was held. We shared in our loss, as our community felt the shockwaves of her gaping absence. I wished that I could have joined her, but I didn't wish that it were me who died – I didn't want her to carry around this kind of horror. Little did I know that she was so much stronger than I ever anticipated.

It took me a while to be ok with putting her ashes into the riverbank. I didn't think of it as her inside the urn, rather feeling like she was already everywhere, but the idea of actually getting rid of her remains hurt my heart. After the spring thaw came, I knew it was the right time. I put her in a backpack and grabbed a collapsible army shovel. There was a park on the edge of the city that she loved. We would take Caligula with us and he would run wild like a beast, clomping through the mud with the echoes of a medieval horse.

There was a spot where the river split off into a creek and formed a mini-peninsula. From here, she could travel down the Mississippi River, crossing through New Orleans, her favorite city, before spreading out into the world. We went at 4:30am, the dog and I, and I began digging the watery sand. After a few minutes, the weathered, old shovel snapped where the head and the handle met, so I found myself digging a hole in the damp, early morning sand with raw, bleeding fingers.

After I dug deep enough, I gently placed her urn into the hole, leaving most of myself with her, buried on the bank. As I covered her, I sobbed until nothing came out but ash. Caligula licked my face and wagged his tail, grumbling for me to toss a stick he had brought over. At the edge of the riverbank, I sat and pondered our life together, all the while tossing the stick for the dog. Like a monk in deep meditation, I sat for hours and hours without moving, other than to throw that damn stick. People came and went, stopping by to see the view of the river, letting their dogs drink from the water. Caligula took every opportunity to play and run, barking as he went, and still I sat.

As the sun got higher, brighter, and the river rose, I could feel her slowly leaving me. Not that her spirit had left, but I knew that her ashes were being spread into the sand, that some were making their way into the flow of the river. Bits of her went up, into the creek, closer to home and deep into the lush green of the park. Other pieces followed the flow of the river, down through the southern part of the state and towards the rest of the country. And once that part of her was done spreading, I could feel her next to me stronger than before, standing on the bank and starting downstream. Not spectral, not physical, but something else. As soon as I could feel it, the warmth of her, breathing in her scent, she was gone.

Caligula and I walked back through the trees and something inside told me that nothing would ever be the same again. Not just for me, not just in my new life – the one I never wanted – no, I could feel in my bones that the world was never going to be the same again.

I crawled my way through the following month, abandoning nearly everything but writing. Nothing felt good, nothing had color or texture; with the loss of her, my life was diminished to mere survival, and barely at that. Caligula got more walks that month than I could count – anything to keep my time occupied, to make myself physically exhausted at the end of the day, enough that I could hopefully sleep. Up to that point, I couldn't bring myself to go back to the river, to visit where I had illegally buried her. It was too much. On the month anniversary of her burial, I loaded up Caligula in the car and headed to the forest, to the river. My Amebix *Arise* tape had been stuck in the tape player for months, "Drink and Be Merry," fittingly, was our soundtrack for most of the drive. I thought we could use some healing, and that maybe she would visit us again.

When we got to the park it was all fenced off. Heavy chains with heavier locks adorned all the gates and there were giant orange signs everywhere warning people not to enter the park grounds. The fences had razor wire with tattered shreds of fur-covered skin and dried, decaying blood. The mystery appealed to me, but I also wanted to go see her; needed to go see her. We walked around the perimeter, well past the path and into the thick brush and dense trees. I wondered how much of the river-bank was fenced off, assuming that the fences ended at, or just into, the water.

We came out the other side of the trees and found the warming sand below our feet. It radiated through my shoes and up into my heels. Somehow, for some reason that I didn't under-stand at the time, they had actually fenced off that entire section of the park, with a long, high fence going into the water a few feet and then following it along the bank. I thought about climbing the fence, but what would I do with Caligula? And that razor wire was not fucking around, either. Here it was also matted with clumps of bloody fur and flesh. In one spot, toxic looking fat dripped down onto the ground and an army of bugs feasted on the drippings.

I turned to leave, heading back into the woods the way we came when a man approached me and asked what we were doing. He wasn't wearing any visible Park Ranger attire, but I figured it was worth talking with him, if only to see if he knew anything about what the fuck was going on here.

He told me about a recent string of animal attacks, maybe some kind of illness that their bites were spreading. Not rabies, it was different, something more sinister. And these weren't just your occasional attack from predatory animals. A woman got half her face bit off by a rabbit. An elderly man, out walking his dog, got attacked by a deer and it ate all the flesh off his arm before some people walking tried to fight it off with rocks; they split its head open and its brains actually oozed out before it ran back into the woods.

I didn't know what to say, obviously. It all sounded so crazy. I wondered if he was just wandering around, peddling conspiracy theories. But then again, he could have been a Parks Department employee. I stared at fresh clump of bloody fur swaying in the gentle breeze for a moment, grateful that this stranger's appearance dissuaded me from trying to climb the fence. I turned to thank him, but he was already a ways away, walking along the bank of the river. I then noticed a silver shine from his back at his beltline; I think he was armed.

I wasn't going to let tales of ravenous, man-eating prey wandering around the park dissuade me from trying to get a little time with her, but that fence was an obvious obstacle. I needed to be near her, so I stepped into the water and followed the chain-link fence to the drop-off point. The fence running along the flow of the river followed closely at the edge of the drop-off, but there was still room for me to balance on it, one hand holding the fence, the other tugging Caligula along with. He was ecstatic in the water, truly his favorite place to be, and now made all the better with me accompanying him.

At about the halfway point, I looked up again, to see if the razor wire was still there, which it was. I had hoped that they didn't string it along the entire top portion of the river side, counting on someone else's laziness to help me out a little. When those hopes were dashed, I considered turning back, but as I was already soaked, I figured I might as well see if they hadn't blocked off the entire peninsula. Another several minutes of balance and grip, I was shocked to find my assumption had been correct. There was about a four-foot by four-foot section just outside of the fence. Someone hadn't considered the growing and shrinking tide line.

Standing there, I realized that was probably pretty close to where I had buried her and a shiver went through my body. As soon as I was done processing it, I was in tears. I could feel my knees give out as I crumpled to the ground, sobbing and gasping for air. Caligula was still splashing around in the water, doing all the dog-stuff that he could. Urgent feelings of guilt and shame shook me, as I apologized to her, to the sand beneath my ass, for abandoning her. Having not visited wrecked me and avoiding coming back here felt like I had let her die all over again. If you ever want to know what the worst part of the worst grief is, at least by my count, it's the guilt. The guilt is the darkness waiting to swallow you whole.

As I wailed, holding myself like an injured child, a cool breeze blew in from the woods; the cold crawled into my bones. My clothes were soaked through, dripping onto the damp peninsula. I was drawn to the comfort of cold, exhausted sleep, but I fought it. My head nodded off a few times, as my eyes continued to leak salt. I anxiously awaited the calm that follows this type of purge, but before it would come I heard three gunshots in the distance. I didn't hesitate getting up to find the source. That level of violence wasn't known to happen at this park, though the possibility didn't surprise me. As I made my way back, along the chain link fence, following the shoreline, I remembered the man with the gun

What if he really was a conspiracy theorist or just a crazy fuck with a gun, possibly shooting wild animals because he believed they were attacking folks, or shooting fucking people's dogs? The thought had me enraged. As soon as I got back onto solid land, Caligula and I took off running towards where I thought the shots came from. The river valley had a way of distorting sound, so I wasn't exactly sure but I gave my best guess. We cut back into the trees. The woods had gone silent in the wake of the noise; all I could hear was my blood pounding in my head, the rhythm of my feet hitting hard-packed dirt, and the gallop of Caligula's stride.

We were about halfway to where I estimated the shots came from, though it could have been anywhere, really, when I heard yelling from the woods ahead. We were on a wide path that cut through the entire park, but we angled into one of the veins that went further into the actual state park that the dog area was connected to. My lungs burned and my side felt like it was devouring itself. Panting and completely out of breath, I stopped to get some air. The yelling got louder, closer, and I could see vague movements from within the gaps in a layer of new green growth upon vibrant brown branches.

I moved forward and pushed the trees away like a curtain. From within the chaos before me, what first struck me was the gun sitting on the ground, like the centerpiece of a Renaissance-era painting, with all the motion occurring around it. Then I saw the three badgers climbing up a shrieking woman. They were taking massive bites out of her flesh. Blood oozed from holes in her tracksuit while she tried to pull them off. She managed to grab one by the back, but when she pulled it, all the fur and flesh slipped off, like a full-body de-gloving. The woman's shrieks got louder and more urgent, but the badger paid no mind to the loss of its skin. It didn't even bleed; there was just a purple slime that glooped off with the hide.

The man who could be a crazy conspiracy theorist or armed Parks Department employee was lying in a puddle of his insides. He looked like he exploded outwards, with a violent spray of congealed crimson surrounding his open torso. Several mangled squirrels gnawed on what appeared to be his spine and shimmering ribs. One was missing all the skin and fur on its face and another was only the front part of a squirrel, with the back end missing completely. The man's hands twitched as inhuman groans escaped his mangled throat.

I tried my best to close the curtain of green, to avoid being seen by these flesh-eating animals. But Caligula had other plans. I don't know if he was initially as shocked as I was, or if it took him a moment to register what he was seeing, or maybe he just didn't know how to react. But as soon as I inched backwards, he lost his goddamn mind. His manic barks were piercing, nauseating.

I was sure that we were about to die, about to join her in whatever comes next. But, I also found myself more than half disappointed when they didn't come after us at all. The growing army of animals stopped to look, but they continued on their macabre feast. I thought about going after the gun, but I didn't want to press my luck – maybe we had just been far enough away that they weren't threatened. But maybe it was something else.

We got out of that park as quickly as we could, running the whole way back to the car. There weren't very many people around, but as we got closer to the entrance to the park I saw a handful of folks. I told them that the park was closed and that they should leave. Only a few listened. I didn't care to stick around and see what happened, so I got Caligula in the car and we headed home.

As I drove, my grief and sorrow made room for the rushing tides of anxiety and bafflement. Only a few blocks from the park section of the park we had been in, I pulled over to compose myself, as I had begun to violently tremble, and I managed to get the door open in time to puke outside of the car, rather than all over myself. Those people were dead, dying. Those animals were...something?

Sitting on the side of the road, I turned off Amebix and silently prayed to her – the only possibly cosmic source that made any sense. Before the words left my brain, I could feel her in my heart and hear her voice in the core of my being. She told me that everything would be ok. She told me that nature was fighting back. I felt her drift away again and a new, endless grief overtook me; I'd lost her again, again. The misery was shattered when I heard screaming coming from the trees to my right. It was then replaced by terror as a horde of wounded, bleeding animals and humans attacked everything in sight.

Small critters, dogs of all sizes, deer, a bear, a few cougars, and a fuck ton of birds, all in various states of wholeness, flocked towards a family sitting on a picnic table. Ribbons of flesh flew through the air as a cloudy pink haze spread in the breeze. By the time the horde was finished, there was scarcely anything left. They dripped small amounts of purple goop behind them as they walked. Some looked relatively normal, but others were missing limbs, had chunks of flesh missing, were missing an eye, or were otherwise fucked.

I struggled to comprehend what I was seeing, when three sparrows flew down and pecked at the face of a young man running towards me, a look of terror on his bleeding face. He swatted at them, shouting and crying as he ran. He managed to pull one of them off, but the bird was still connected with its small talons and beak. As he wrenched it away from his bloody cheek, it tore chunks of stretchy skin and fat away with it. He fast-pitched it against a tree and it exploded into a burst of feathers and opaque, purple jelly.

He managed to get away from the other two, but as he ran his steps became erratic, jumpy. Three dogs had started to chase, but they abruptly turned back in search of other prey. The terror and pain that had painted his face was replaced by an ominous and vacant expression. He sniffed at the air and then, without notice, he locked eyes with me and a crooked snarl made its way across his mangled face. The bleeding on his open face wounds had stopped and the blood had transformed into the same gloopy, purple slime.

I fixated on the transformative process from blood to purple goo and before I even noticed that he had moved, he was skulking outside of the car, shrieking and trying to punch through the window. Caligula lost his shit, manically barking and growling demonically. I struggled to turn the keys, to get the motor running so I could get away from the fucked up man with the fucked up face and all the fucked up animals, but my hands were clumsy, slow. As he lifted his fists to strike the window again, the three dogs from before, mangy and broken, pulled him to the ground, into the pile of vomit, and tore his body into pieces.

They paid us no mind, and once again went running off towards a family on bikes who were all screaming, having clearly taken the wrong bike path. The dogs made fast work of them, as did a growing collection of beast and man alike. I tore myself from the grips of fear and my hands answered when I told them to move. I started the car and we drove as fast as we could until the river valley was a distant memory. But the fear and confusion remained.

Moving on instinct, I hadn't been paying the greatest attention to what was happening around me until I found myself in the thick of a traffic jam. I tried my best to breathe, to not freak out at what had happened, when I saw people running. Fighting against the sour in my stomach, my mind battled against the truth of why people were running.

It was the human creatures first. I had no idea how they had gotten here, but they were spreading, violently and impossibly fast. From the seat of the car, I watched these monsters brutalize and mangle people at random. They were grabbing those who were fleeing, tearing unsuspecting motorists from their cars, and pulling people off their bikes and biting into their flesh. Those who weren't too damaged quickly joined the horde and participated in the orgy of death with them.

They were still a little ways up the road, so I got Caligula and we abandoned the car, like so many others had. I didn't know where to go, so we just ran, avoiding clusters of these undead as best as we could. We ended up at the playground of a school. It looked mostly empty, but when we turned the corner of the building, there was an ocean of them. The only thing I could think to do was climb to the highest point of the playground equipment, so I grabbed all 37 pounds of the dog and ran as fast as I could, while the ocean of dead rushed towards me.

I got to the top of the playground equipment, but all that

meant was sitting atop the highest point on the tube-slide. I had nothing to fight with and couldn't set the dog down. There was no way that I wasn't completely fucked. As they charged, I felt her once again. My heart was filled with warmth and love, as her voice radiated around me, shaking my trembling flesh. She told me that the world as it had been was over. In death, she built a new one. Soon the dead would dry out and die again, but not before they toppled civilization. Through her, they would reset the world and let it breathe again.

As she spoke, softly but with such power behind it, I could see my body being carried away by the mob of undead. I was being shredded into snapping tendons, broken bones, and tearing flesh. Yet some other part of me remained on the slide, holding some other part of Caligula. She told me that she was sorry; she didn't know that she wouldn't be able to control the humans. She hadn't intended on me dying so suddenly, as I hadn't with her. I looked up and saw a black sun and the bleeding moon and I knew all we had to do was let go; let go and let nature take its course.

ABOUT THE EDITOR & AUTHORS

Sam Richard is a writer and the co-editor of Hybrid Moments: A Literary Tribute to the Misfits and Blood for You: A Literary Tribute to GG Allin. His writing has appeared in such varied publications as NihilismRevised's Strange Behaviors: An Anthology of Absolute Luridity, Clash Magazine, The Junk Merchants: A Literary Salute to William S. Burroughs, Dark Moon Digest, and Splatterpunk Zine, among many others. He is primarily focused on writing weird horror with an emphasis on grief. Recently a widower, he slowly rots in Minneapolis, MN, and is accessible on any number of social media platforms.

David W. Barbee is an author of bizarro, weird, strange, cool, awesome, and totally effed up fiction. His work is full of dark monsters and strange maniacs, influenced by a deranged child-hood diet of cartoons, comic books, and cult movies. He is the author of BACON FRIED BASTARD, THE NIGHT'S NEON FANGS, THUNDERPUSSY, and the Wonderland award-nominated A TOWN CALLED SUCKHOLE. He lives in the mangy wilderness of Georgia, next door to one of the world's most polluting power plants.

While in high school, **Asher Ellis** was introduced to punk music, in part, by the 1998 film, SLC Punk. Ellis would later go on to release his debut horror novel, The Remedy, published by Full Fathom Five in 2015. Seventeen years after SLC Punk's protagonist, Stevo, explained the differences between punks and "posers," The Remedy introduced the character of Rob, who Ellis is sure Stevo would've referred to as "a trendy fuck."

Axel Kohagen is a writer from Minneapolis, MN. With Roy C. Booth, he is the author of several horrific short stories including "Last Stop," "Just Another Ex," and "The Most Wonderful Undead Time of the Year." Under his own byline, he has a story published in Human Cuisine, and defined "horror" and "Stephen King" for The Encyclopedia of Men and Masculinities. His work has been mentioned in Rue Morgue Magazine. Axel has seen Skinny Puppy in concert three times and still remembers buying copies of Industrial Nation in Iowa City.

Emma Alice Johnson writes stories and books and zines. She lifts weights and eats candy. She has only fought a zombie once in real life. She lives in Minneapolis by the lakes.

Madison McSweeney is a Canadian writer and poet. A genre fiction enthusiast and lifelong rock fan, she frequently covers the arts, music, and local horror scenes as a freelance writer. Her nonfiction has appeared in The Fulcrum, Bravewords, Music Vice, and Hellbound, as well as her personal blog (rantsandwritingsblog. wordpress.com).She has previously explored the zombie apocalypse in her story "We Have Rules Here," which appeared in Elder Signs Press' Dark Horizons: An Anthology of Dark Science Fiction."Punk Poem," her poetic tribute to the Ramones, appeared in The Fulcrum in May 2017.

Nicholaus Patnaude's illustrated novel, First Aide Medicine, was published by Emergency Press. His second book, entitled Guitar Wolf, was published by Eraserhead Press. He also serves as editor-in-chief at Psychedelic Horror Press. Punk altered his worldview at an early age, inspiring his DIY approach to writing, publishing, and art. I Walked With A Zombie is one of his favorite films.

Joe Quenell grew up playing in various subpar punk bands. He quit those bands to focus on writing subpar stories. As a teenager he used to worship at the altars of Romero and Fulci, but lately he'd rather re-watch Return of the Living Dead. He lives in Washington State with his partner. "I am the Future" is his first published story.

Sam Reeve is a writer and artist based in Vancouver, Canada. At age 10 she attended her very first show at a local church – the Christian pop punk and ska bands Relient K and DayzWage. Since then she's graduated to much harder and secular stuff, and is currently awaiting surgery on her wrist for a mosh pit injury sustained at an Oi Polloi show in 2012. Her fiction has also appeared in the anthology Dead Bait 4 from Severed Press.

Leo X. Robertson is a Scottish process engineer and emerging writer, currently living in Oslo, Norway. While he is an orderly chap who enjoys thermodynamics, pajamas and a work-life balance, zombie punks riot in his heart. He has work most recently published by Helios Quarterly, Unnerving Magazine, Open Pen and Psychedelic Horror Press, among others. Find him on Twitter @Leoxwrite or check out his website: leoxrobertson.wordpress.com

Danger Slater is the world's most flammable writer. Seriously, he's about to burst into flames. He saw his first punk show at the age of 14, wherein he was kicked in the teeth and fell forever in love. You can find his books I Will Rot Without You, Puppet Skin, and He Digs a Hole through Fungasm Press. He lives in Portland, OR, and his favorite zombie movie is Dead Alive.

Brendan Vidito is a short story author and novelist from Sudbury, Ontario. His work has appeared in several places including Dark Moon Digest, Tragedy Queens: Stories Inspired by Lana Del Rey and Sylvia Plath, and Dead Bait 4. He also writes about horror movies for Clash Media. His partner plays drums in an all-girl punk band. He once drunkenly vowed never to write about ghosts, zombies or vampires. He already broke that vow. Twice. He's hoping the inevitable vampire story will make him rich. You can visit him at brendanvidito.wordpress.com.

Carmilla Voiez is a Goth-Aspie-Anarchist who writes about oppression, gender and class through the lens of horror. As a lover of punk music and an admirer of Romero, she doesn't allow her "zombies" to be distracted by sky-flowers. Born in Bristol (England) in the 70s, she now lives in N.E. Scotland. Other work includes self-published novels "The Ballerina and the Revolutionary" and "The Starblood Trilogy", "Starblood, the graphic novel" and a collection of short stories "Broken Mirror and Other Morbid Tales." Her blog and samples of her work can be found at www.carmillavoiez.com.

Mark Zirbel lives and writes in Milwaukee, Wisconsin. His horror and bizarro fiction has appeared in numerous publications, such as Peep Show Volumes 1 and 2, Morpheus Tales: The Best Weird Fiction Volume 1, Cthulhu Unbound Volume 2, Dead Bait, Bare Bone #10, Chimeraworld 4, and DeathGrip: Exit Laughing. Mark is no stranger to punk-themed fiction, as his story "Slice-and-Grab" was featured in Weirdpunk Books' Hybrid Moments: A Literary Tribute to the Misfits. However, despite appearing in more than 20 anthologies and magazines in the U.S., U.K., and Australia, this is Mark's first published zombie story. George Romero be praised!

ALSO BY CLASH BOOKS

TRAGEDY QUEENS: STORIES INSPIRED BY LANA DEL REY & SYLVIA PLATH

edited by Leza Cantoral

DARK MOONS RISING IN A STARLESS NIGHT

Mame Bougouma Diene

NOHO GLOAMING & THE CURIOUS CODA OF ANTHONY SANTOS

Daniel Knauf (Creator of HBO's Carnivàle)

IF YOU DIED TOMORROW I WOULD EAT YOUR CORPSE

Wrath James White

GIRL LIKE A BOMB

Autumn Christian

THE ANARCHIST KOSHER COOKBOOK

Maxwell Bauman

HORROR FILM POEMS

Christoph Paul

NIGHTMARES IN ECTASY

Brendan Vidito

THE VERY INEFFECTIVE HAUNTED HOUSE

Jeff Burk

HE HAS MANY NAMES

Drew Chial

CENOTE CITY

Monique Quintana

THIS BOOK AIN'T NUTTIN TO FUCK WITH: A WU-TANG TRIBUTE ANTHOLOGY

edited by Christoph Paul & Grant Wamack